Return to Portlyon

Blythe Robinson

To my wonderful husband, and our Cornish summers together

ACKNOWLEDGMENTS

Thanks to Teresa, who convinced me that my stories were worth telling and I could be the one to do it. To Jane Rayner, Anna, Cass, and Kate for your critical friendship and editorial experience. And to Mia, Neil, and Emma for your support, enthusiasm, and shared love of romance

1 BITTER-SWEET

"I don't want to have to deal with this!"

Lizbeth McCleary waved an arm, clad in vintage Celia Birtwell fabric, towards her daughter and pressed the button of her smoothie maker. The green froth pulsed. She decanted the goop into a tall glass and finished it off with a stick of celery.

Jessica Trelawny watched her mother fondly, an amused expression on her face. Lizbeth took a swig of her concoction and grimaced. She had blitzed up kale, watercress, kiwi fruit, and coconut water.

"Now you're laughing at me," she pointed an accusatory celery stalk at Jessica and took another swig. She pulled a face again, "Ugh, bitter – too much kale."

"I am *not* laughing at you," Jess held her hands up, innocently. "Mother, you know I take you very seriously. Always."

"How that man haunts me still, after so many years!"

"Well, you did have a child with him – me!"

Lizbeth walked around the marble-topped island in her well-appointed, rustic-seeming London kitchen.

"*You* are the best thing that man and I ever produced. We were good together for long enough and nothing – nothing – that came after that can spoil it!"

Jess knew that for all her mother's drama, Lizbeth was sincere with this. She adored her daughter and the feeling was mutual. She looked deep into Jess's eyes, the same pale blue as her own. "You deserve this, darling, you deserve a fresh start and a new opportunity like this."

Looking at all her belongings packed in boxes, Jess marveled at how much clutter she had managed to squeeze into a tiny one-bedroom flat in West London over four years. She trotted down the stairs and out into the courtyard below. In the corner shop she bought some fruit pastilles and a couple of magazines. She ran her fingers through her shoulder-length dirty-blonde curls as she stood outside on the pavement. Mostly, she hated how her naturally curly hair made her look unruly and messy, or out of fashion.

A honk. A high-top van pulled up alongside her. She waved at the driver. She was all set for the journey to Cornwall with Alastair. Tradition dictated that she had fruit pastilles and magazines for the long drive.

Alastair was her mother's close 'friend'. He made short work of loading her belongings and soon they were heading westwards out of the city and into the late evening traffic for the overnight journey. As the miles disappeared, Jess and Alastair sang along to the Classic Hits station, playing familiar songs of the 1960s, 70s, and 80s. This took her back to the journeys of her childhood with her mother. In those days, they made the day-long trip to Cornwall in Lizbeth's old Morris Minor Traveller, to the rugged cliffs and the winding cobbled lanes of Portlyon.

Portlyon, lovely, longed-for Portlyon. The harbour town where Jess's famous father, artist Kristof Trelawny, had resided for twenty years. Kristof was once the *enfant terrible* of the 1970s art scene. He relocated to Portlyon in the 1980s and reinvented his whole style and approach. From angry abstracts he had turned to Cornish weather scenes with bobbing, colourful fishing boats and cloudy skies dotted with herring gulls. By the time he passed away, a few months ago, his 'Seasons in Portlyon' series had graced many a tea-towel, jigsaw puzzle, and drinks coaster in gift shops the length and breadth of Cornwall.

Jess stared out of the window of the van. Her whole life was packed in the back of the vehicle. Her thoughts drifted back to summers in Portlyon. They had been full and eventful. Friendly people and smiling faces. It was the only time she had spent with Kristof, her summertime, part-time father. Down by the small, busy harbour he had a studio in the old Sailmaker's Loft. He lived downstairs and worked upstairs in a large, light, airy room. He drew and painted prolifically, and hosted his only daughter, once a year, for a memorable summer.

Now, all of it belonged to her.

When the news of Kristof's death reached her she was working her usual twelve-hour shift at 'The Centre', the most fashionable eatery in Covent Garden. With a cleaver in one hand and her phone in the other she listened to Lizbeth sobbing at her. She had told her mother not to cry, as she quietly processed her own feelings.
With this thought, and the memories of her father, she dozed off to the steady hum of the traffic.

"Jess – Jessica," Alastair shook her shoulder and killed the engine. "We're here."
"What?" she inhaled sharply as she roused herself. Jess could sleep very deeply thanks to a life of long, hard shifts in restaurants.
"We're here, Portlyon," he smiled and got out of the cab to open the back of the truck.
Jess rubbed her eyes and yawned. She climbed down and stood to survey the old familiar scene. There was Portlyon, hardly altered since the last time. When was it? At age fifteen? Fifteen summers ago. The Portlyon seaside smell and the glistening blue-sapphire light on the sea at night.

Inside the Sailmaker's Loft studio, she unpacked the kettle from the first of the boxes and switched the water on under the sink. The pipes thudded and groaned after years of misuse and some rusty-coloured water sputtered out of the brass tap over the old ceramic sink. Once it ran clear, she filled the kettle and switched on the bottled gas by the hob.

She made her way outside onto the deck that wrapped around the Loft, a cup of steaming green tea cradled in her hands. The very earliest glimmers of dawn began to appear and touch the waves as the stars disappeared above her. Alastair slept downstairs on the old sofa in front of the wood-burner. Jess took the chance to spend some time alone in her father's old studio. Now outside, she shivered and checked her watch, four-thirty in the morning. She pulled her baggy cardigan around her shoulders.

From her vantage point, she could see and hear the fishermen on the boats below as they arrived with their catch of herring from out in the Celtic Sea. They called out to one another as the blue light from the sheds at the harbour caught their features in the shadows. As they packed the catch into more fresh ice she saw their breath in the chilly air of a September dawn. She felt relaxed and sipped her hot tea. The warm glow of the lamp in the studio behind her silhouetted her against the sky.

One of the fishermen down below looked up briefly, then he paused in his work. She had a sense that he was watching her, taking her in. He turned to one of his fellows and seemed to say something funny because his three companions burst out laughing. One of them clapped the joker on the back. Jess felt her colour rise, self-conscious even in the dim morning light. She re-entered the shelter of the studio loft and closed the shutters. She was unsure why she felt so embarrassed. She did not know these people and it was not as if she could say the joke was directed at her.

The embarrassment might stem from the fact that the fisherman had a confident, energetic strength, almost a swagger, as he heaved the boxes of fresh catch into stacks on the quay. Jess curled up under a warm shawl on the studio's double divan bed. She heard the wash of the sea as she drifted off to sleep and thought about a pair of strong shoulders in a warm woollen sweater, as the gulls cried in the distance.

2 FRESH START

Jess awoke a few hours later to the patter and screech of the gulls. They seemed to be having a fight on the flat roof of the studio.

Alastair soon joined her, to finish unloading the boxes from the van and after they had shifted most of the heavy stuff together Jess went in search of ingredients. Soon, the scent of breakfast filled the Loft. She had found an excellent butcher's, on a side street, that sold locally sourced dry-cured back bacon and free-range eggs. The bakery nearby offered a fresh batch of warm sourdough loaves on its trays. She was thrilled with the deli that had its own roastery for fresh coffee beans.
Jess sat Alastair down to a sumptuous meal of eggs benedict topped with crispy bacon on griddled sourdough, finished off with a drizzle of basil oil. She never went anywhere without her utensils, kitchen tools, and range of larder ingredients, many of them her own custom version and recipe. After the kettle and tea-bags these were the items she unpacked.

Alastair leaned back from the table with a satisfied sigh. His salt and pepper beard sported sourdough crumbs and his plate was scoured clean.
"Jess, girl, I shall miss your cooking!"
She laughed, "You and Mum will always be welcome here at a moment's notice. Especially as I shall need a really good handyman and I don't know anyone here yet."
And, she thought to herself, she would miss his cheerfulness and South London banter. Also, without the influence of retired cabbie

Alastair, her mother's company could sometimes – how should she put it? – become wearisome.

"I'm so glad she has you. It makes the move here so much easier."

"Well," he looked a little embarrassed, "your Ma and I, we're good friends."

"Al," she placed a small hand gently on his large workman's hand, "I know you two are more than just 'friends'. You've been an item for ages and I'm pleased. You both deserve to be happy."

"How long have you known?"

"Oh, about two years – longer – you're not all that good at keeping secrets."

"Your mother," he spoke quietly, sincerely, his pale eyes a little watery, "is a very special lady. I wouldn't want you to think I'm taking advantage or nothing. It's just that she's not ready to …".

"Make an honest man of you?" Jess finished when he paused.

The big man laughed. "But she's been hurt – *you* know – so she wanted to take things slow, be sure."

"I understand. After everything my dad meant to her and then everything he put her through, she's always been cautious. But I know you'll be there for her. You're not like him in any way!"

Later, Jess waved Alastair off with bacon butties for the journey back to London. He had enveloped her in one of his customary huge hugs with the promise that he would visit again soon to help her out. He honked the horn and turned left at the bottom of the road and with a wave he was gone. She turned back to the Loft and mounted the stairs to the studio. The planks and weatherboard of the Sailmaker's Yard and Loft were beautifully blistered and peeling with ages of blue-turquoise and clotted-cream coloured paint. These were the seaside colours of her childhood.

Inside, the steeply pitched beamed ceiling and rafters were also painted white and cream. A set of double doors let out onto the surrounding deck. Throughout this upper floor were windows that let in the maximum light all year round. A pair of skylights added to the open feeling. Along one side was a series of cupboards and a basic kitchenette. At one end of the large room was a curtained bathroom, no more than a shower cubicle and a loo. From floor to ceiling, surrounding the double studio divan in the centre of the room, were Jess's boxes and suitcases. She had all her equipment, of course, plus her cookbooks, and her functional wardrobe. This mostly consisted of work clothes, jeans, and the occasional interesting item for clubbing. Hers was a collection of necessities, the opposite of her mother's exquisite vintage textiles and designer wear.

She tore the tape off one of the boxes, labelled 'Boots and Shoes – outdoor', and took out a pair of dilapidated trainers. Instead of unpacking today she decided to explore and see if any of her old haunts were the same. After all, this was her home now and, for better or worse, she wanted to get on with things. She laced up her trainers and pulled on a pair of distressed denim shorts and her favourite Debbie Harry tour t-shirt. Her hair, messy as usual, she twisted into a bun. Immediately, unruly tendrils and curls escaped from it. Locking up the studio she trotted down the stairs and into the sunshine of a late September day.

The town of Portlyon was quiet. The dense tourist traffic had departed and left it to the locals only a couple of weeks earlier. Jess breathed the fresh air and caught the scent of the sea once again. 'I know I'll never get tired of this,' she thought. Her new life was just beginning.

London had been great, for career and friends, but there had always been something missing for her. She had been searching for a goal and at thirty-one, felt this was the time to take some chances for herself. After Kristof's death his will had come as a huge shock for her. He had two sons from his first marriage and two sons from his third marriage. Jess was the middle child to his second wife, Lizbeth. At the funeral they had a reunion of sorts, never having really known one another. The younger children and his widow, Maxine, had come over from France, his final home. He was laid to rest in Highgate cemetery alongside other notable writers, artists, and politicians. A man of the age.

7

The Sunday papers had tried to find the scandal amongst the attendees at the funeral: the feuding ex-wives, the many children, the possible conflict over the estate of 'England's Picasso'. Jess had stood apart. She had not been a member of the eldest Hampstead-born family, the sons Hugo and Jeremy, who now worked in the city and the media. Neither was she a member of the autumn-winter brood of his later life, Christophe and Sebastian, the young children of the warm South. No, Jess was the awkward middle-child of Kristof's summertime rebellion as he tried to cling on to his youth and notoriety when he felt middle-age set in. His flamboyant years had needed a flamboyant wife.

Lizbeth was an artist and designer greatly in demand. They had made the perfect bohemian couple. Married in the Chelsea registry office they had run away together. Re-surfacing in Portlyon, theirs had been a grand passion that burned brightly and intensely. Jess was the product of this union, the wide-eyed baby with the tousled hair. The brief, electric marriage had left Lizbeth scarred and angry but she had doggedly rebuilt her life. She became a textile designer popular with the large fashion houses, and she gave Jess an artistic upbringing of theatre, gallery openings, and Soho café life.

One summer, unexpectedly, Kristof asked if she wanted to spend the holidays with him. She was nine and only had a slight idea of who her father was. He requested the 'pleasure of her company' for a summer in Cornwall. Mostly out of curiosity, she agreed. Lizbeth and she drove down to Portlyon in the noisy Morris Traveller, windows down with Kate Bush on the tape deck. Lizbeth and Kristof greeted one another coolly and from that point on, and for the next six years, Jess was his summertime daughter. Sunburnt cheeks and sand between her toes.

It had been a grand experience. She would wait for the train, with sandwiches packed and suitcase bursting, or sit beside her mother on the clackety drive down. Kristof was always pleased to see her, always ready to host her, with carefully planned activities. She gradually grew devoted to him. She lived downstairs, amidst paint pots and canvasses. She spent the morning in his studio upstairs as

8

he worked. Then she would race barefoot along the sands of nearby Penlyon Cove, sheltered by tall jagged cliffs on either side. She played in and out of the water all day long with the local children, and then Kristof carried her home, sleepy and freckled, to the Loft. She slept on the studio divan whilst he painted.

One sad summer, after six years, it had all come to an end. An abrupt call to her mother and Kristof was gone, no longer hers for the long Cornish summers. He had a new wife, already pregnant, and moved to France to paint and sculpt in the Mediterranean sun.

Lizbeth helped her through it.
"This is what he does," she comforted. "I'm so sorry you had to find out like this. He leaves. He makes you the centre of his universe and then he leaves. I wish I had never let him back into your life."
Jess told her not to blame herself.
She had been able to re-focus with school and London life. After a couple of years, the blissful summers were a thing of the past, carried away like the scudding clouds across the water, along with any notion of having a father in her life.

It was, therefore, with a sense of astonishment that she had heard Kristof's Last Will and Testament. He left her the property in Cornwall, Sailmaker's Loft, and all its contents. Those contents, it turned out, were a mildewed shower curtain decorated with sailing boats, some old green crockery, a chipped milk jug, a lot of mouse droppings, and some empty paint cans. But, nevertheless, this was all hers, and it was sound. He had remembered her at the end. She decided to move her life there with the money from her tiny London flat. She would work hard to work out her dreams and try to achieve them.

On this bright morning, Jess made her way through the town and up onto the cliff path. She looked down at the sparkling water of Penlyon Cove. Above her were rows of bright, charming cottages and elegant Victorian seaside villas climbing up the hillside. Below, she could look out over the sparkling waters of the Cove and beyond that to the fishing boats bobbing in Portlyon Harbour.

Her thoughts drifted back to the previous night, and the handsome fisherman highlighted out of the shadows on the harbourside, his deep laugh and relaxed banter. She stood on tiptoe and let the wind blow against her, goose-bumps prickled up her bare legs.

Powerful hands grabbed her arms from behind and she was spun around, roughly. The breath knocked from her lungs.

"What the bloody hell are you doing?"

3 REUNIONS

Jess looked up into a pair of angry, dark eyes with thick frowning brows above them. Dark hair, tousled and messy like her own, was blown by the clifftop breeze.

Too surprised to speak yet, she took a deep breath as he dragged her away from the edge. She felt strong fingers digging into the flesh of her upper arms. She saw a pair of muscular shoulders and sensed an overwhelming masculine scent.

"Ow!" she managed to complain. "Let go!"

He released her and she rubbed her arms where red fingermarks had begun to stand out on her pale skin. His hands brushed the line of her hips and she leaned into him for balance – instinctively. She regained control.

"Sorry," his voice was deep, still irritated, "but what were you doing leaning over the edge like that?"

"I wasn't leaning," she spoke curtly in reply, trying to regain her composure. He was having an effect on her that she had to try to control. "I was just feeling the breeze," she knew this sounded rather lame.

"Oh – feeling the breeze? Is that right?" He expressed some angry sarcasm and she could see the strong line of his jaw clench. "Feeling the breeze but not reading the signs," and he pointed to the low-level warning notice near their feet. It read: 'Danger of Subsidence. Keep Clear'. For emphasis, there was a little picture of a man falling and some tumbling rocks.

"Well," she felt stupid, "I didn't see that – but I was hardly near the edge!" She was able to take in the sight of him now. Taller than her, broad shoulders with a slim waist, he wore faded jeans and a sturdy pair of walking boots, a plain grey t-shirt with a plaid work-shirt tied

11

around his waist. In an instant she recognised him as the joker from the harbour in the early hours of the morning. She felt herself begin to blush. He noticed.

"So," she said, flustered. "I should thank you, I suppose." She just wanted to get away from him now.

"Wait," he reached for her hand, concerned, "lots of tourists get into difficulty on the cliff paths. Are you sure you're ok?"

She looked at his hand. A hard-working strong hand, but she refused it.

"I'm not a tourist," she shot back, and then turned on her heel and ran down the path in the direction of the town.

"What?" She heard him call after her, "You *live* here?"

Jess glanced back at him, quickly, to make sure he was not following her. She slowed up and breathed a little easier as the distance between them grew. He stood on the clifftop, hands on hips, watching her stride away.

Once she reached the vicinity of the Sailmaker's Yard, her feelings began to calm. She arrived at the Loft. A woman in a brightly coloured headscarf, with a large handbag, a red mackintosh, and blue pastel shoes greeted her joyously. She had been applying lipstick using a 1950s-style vintage compact and spotted Jess in the mirror. She turned around, her arms flung wide.

"You came! You're here!" she beamed a freshly crimsoned smile and threw her arms around Jess. The woman then pulled away and examined her face, closely.

"Are you ok? You seem a little – out of sorts – flushed."

The stranger placed a palm on Jess's forehead in a maternal fashion. "My," she held her at arms' length, "but you do look so much like him!" She beamed at Jess again. "Jessica – don't you remember me?"

The woman whipped off her headscarf to expose a cascading torrent of henna-coloured curls. They matched the lipstick and the mackintosh.

Jess looked at her curiously, and then noticed a white push-bike with a green wicker basket on the front propped against the wooden railing.

"Aunt Matty?" it came flooding back to her. "It's so good to see you!"

They hugged each other excitedly.

Jess's Aunt Mathilde Trelawny, Kristof's sister, escorted her into the Loft and then, immediately, burst into tears.

"Oh, but he loved his time with you here so much!" She took the young woman's face in her well-manicured hands and kissed her, a lip-stick mark tattooed Jess's cheek.

"Don't cry, oh please don't cry," Jess wiped her aunt's eyes, and her own cheek. She put the kettle on.

"No, no, I have something *much* better," and she drew from her capacious handbag a bottle of champagne.

"This is your housewarming, after all. Got any glasses?"

The aunt and niece sat beside one of the large open windows in the Loft and drank warm champagne out of coffee mugs. They looked down over the harbour scene and reminisced about the summers Jess had spent there. Mathilde had been the loving figure who supplied picnic food, fishing nets, sticking plasters, and hugs. She took Jess rock-pooling and for ice-cream whilst Kristof sketched, and made generous dinners and barbecues at the end of long, summer evenings. With her, Jess had tasted her first cider at fourteen. Aunt Matty had no children of her own and she put her all into helping her brother provide Jess with memorable holidays. They were precious family times for her.

"I have missed you *so* much over the years. I was so mad at Kristof when he finished it all and left like that. I know you and your mother must have been so hurt by that. She called me – it must be years since we had spoken – and told me the good news. You were coming back! She asked me to look out for you and help you if I can. I said, I couldn't wait! Anything you need – anything at all – just ask."

Aunt Matty ran on in this fashion.

Jess smiled and listened.

Out of the corner of her eye, as her aunt talked, she caught a flash of a check shirt down at the harbour-side. She did not look round, at first. But then, like a string that pulled at her, she turned her head

13

and found herself watching the joker, now her strange unwelcome protector, whilst she sipped on her elevenses mug of champagne.

He stood, holding a set of empty crates, laughing as usual with another fisherman who was threading some lobster pots together. In the glinting sunshine they joked and chatted, their Cornish burr reached her at the window. Her joker moved carefully about the deck of his fishing boat. She noticed the name, 'Carrie-Ann'. Probably his wife, she thought. He had a good smile and a good, deep laugh. She liked the sound of his laugh, as long as it was not directed at her.

Mathilde had stopped speaking.
She coughed politely at her niece, "You certainly don't waste any time!"
"Huh?" Jess turned back to her.
"Eyeing up the local talent, I see!"
"What? No! I just thought I recognised someone."
"Really? After all these years, isn't that wonderful! Who is it?"

Colourful Mathilde perched at the window and looked out. It was as if a bird of paradise was displaying on the upper deck, and there was no way the fishermen below could miss seeing her. Jess blushed furiously again, and rose quickly to grab the champagne bottle from the table.
"Aunty, please don't do this!"
"Do what?" Matty knelt by the sill of the open window. "Who caught your eye? Johnny? No. Or Bill? Couldn't be him. They're not your type, I suspect!" She spoke sideways in a mock confidential tone to her niece. Jess made herself as small as possible and busy at the kitchenette.
"It must be Rob – Rob Tredegar!"
To her horror, Jess saw the joker in the check shirt look up at the mention of his name. He shielded his eyes from the early autumn sunshine as Mathilde gestured to him.
"Yoo hoo! Rob, up here!"
"*Matty*!" Jess muttered to her between clenched teeth.

14

"There's no harm, darling. He's a lovely boy!" She continued, "Yoo hoo! Come on up."

Jess thought, 'Who *actually* says Yoo hoo?'

Rob pointed to his chest and mouthed, "Me?"

"Robert!" "Young Rob!" The other fishermen playfully gibed him. "Looks like you're a hit with the ladies."

Jess's heart pounded in her chest. She heard him run around the quay. Rob, Robert Tredegar is his name. His footsteps drew closer, up the wooden stairs. The door opened and he walked into the studio.

"Rob!" Aunt Matty embraced him and planted her lipstick brand on his cheek. It was Rob's turn to blush and feel awkward as he gingerly returned the hug.

"Another glass, Jessica! I mean a mug," she laughed, "for the lovely Rob." Her aunt escorted him to sit down beside her on the window seat.

Jess reached for another mug from one of her boxes, trying her best to be casual, even nonchalant. She filled it with champagne and handed it to him. Rob took it, with an awkward, shy demeanour. Then she realised it was a white mug bearing a vibrant red heart and the words 'Sexy' and 'Hot Stuff' scrawled across it. It had been a jokey 'Secret Valentine' present from a fellow singleton at work. Chefs and sous chefs found it hard to date.

Rob looked at the mug, raised an eyebrow, and raised the drink, "Cheers, welcome to Portlyon," he pronounced it 'Port-lee-on' in his Cornish accent. "So, you were telling the truth, you aren't a tourist."

"You've already met?" Matty had a mischievous glint in her eye.

"Our paths – crossed," Jess spoke quietly and swigged from her mug. She gave him an embarrassed glance.

"Yes," he spoke politely, "we ran into each other. So, you're new to the town." He looked around the Loft. "It's been a long time since I've been in this place."

15

Jess noticed his strong, tanned fingers holding the mug, his other hand stuffed in the pocket of his faded jeans. Tight jeans. His shirt was stretched across his muscular shoulders. His complexion was a year-round tan, weather-beaten, with slight creases at the corners of his eyes when he smiled, which was often. A few grey hairs touched the dark ones at his temples.

Jess looked away, quickly, afraid he would notice how much she was scrutinising him.

Rob chatted to Mathilde, "I used to do some odd-jobs for the old fella who lived here, when I was a teenager." He walked over to the windows along one side, "I painted these frames and – yes fixed this pane when it was broken."

"And," declared Matty, smiling mischievously again, "that means you two *have* met before, a *long* time ago."

Rob and Jess looked at each other. Jess wanted to look into his eyes forever.

"Jessica used to spend her summers here, when she was a girl," Matty hugged her niece.

Rob fixed her with his dark eyes. She knew she blushed under his gaze.

"*You're* little Jessie? I remember you! When I painted the outside of the Loft you used to follow me around every day. You pestered the life out of me. What were you? Ten? So, your dad was Kris, the artist?"

"Yes!" Mathilde laughed. "We used to picnic on the deck at the end of the day."

"I loved that," he had started to relax now as he reminisced. He looked at Jess, "And you had those pink plastic sandals that you were so proud of. *And* your face was always covered with ice cream."

Jess now realised she had to halt this trip down memory lane. Before she could say anything, however, the pager clipped to Rob's belt bleeped. She had not noticed it before. It was a small black pager with a digital display. *RNLI Lifeboats* with the fluttering red and white flag logo was displayed on one side. He looked at the message. "Got to go. A shout."

16

Jess felt a sense of relief that he was about to go. She had been on edge ever since he walked in. But she also knew that something serious was in the air.

"Oh Lordy," Matty patted his back. "Take care!"

Just as he was about to go, Rob turned, "Tomorrow night, the Folk Club down the hill. Fallon's throwing an engagement party – see you *both* there."

He made eye contact with Jess, and then he was gone.

"Local lifeboat," Matty explained as Rob's footsteps pounded down the stairs and onto the quay. "Rob's the coxswain, the youngest we've ever had out of Portlyon. Someone must be in trouble on the cliffs or out at sea."

Jess looked out of the window, at the crew members responding to the shout. That explained his behaviour to her on the clifftop. Why he took it so personally, as if he had a duty towards her. A lifeboat skipper concerned for her safety.

"A painting party," Matty interrupted her thoughts, "that's what we'll have – to really tart the place up!" Her aunt hugged her again.

Jess looked out across the harbour. 'He's having an engagement party tomorrow', she thought. 'My timing was always lousy'.

17

4 UNTAMED

Jess applied some muted gloss onto her lower lip and smacked her lips together in the cracked mirror above the basin in the shower room. Next, she used a sweep of blusher and some mascara for a little definition. Nothing too heavy, keep it simple, natural. She stepped back and tousled her hair. Then she stopped and sighed. "What's the point?" she asked aloud. "Maybe, tame it?"

She knew she had some straighteners in a box somewhere. An ex-boyfriend had bought her some a few years ago, because he told her she would look better with straight hair. He preferred it. If only she had straight hair, then things would have been fine. It would have worked out. After buying her the hair straighteners he had dumped her over cocktails at a Park Lane hotel. He left her with the bill. It had taken her so long to try and sort her hair out before the date that she was over half an hour late. He disliked tardiness more than he disliked curly hair.

She decided not to be late tonight and leave her hair as it was. Aunt Matty would arrive at any moment. Jess had settled on a simple shift dress, with an abstract pattern in green and white. It was one of Lizbeth's choices, in fact. A rare item – a dress – in Jess's wardrobe, but thanks to her mother's insistence she had bought this one. She teamed it with a pair of simple leather flats in teal.

Matty knocked on the door, then let herself in. Jess had drawn the faded linen blinds throughout the studio living space.
"I come bearing gifts!" Matty held up another bottle. This time the white wine was chilled. "You look lovely," she held Jess's hands and

18

span her around. "Very dressy – for the Folk Club. You'll be the belle of the ball."

"Oh – no – I'll change," Jess earnestly did not want to stand out and draw attention to her herself. In any case, she thought, this was an engagement party for Rob and a woman called Fallon.

"Nonsense," said her aunt, "it's about time someone showed a little class around this place. Now, bottoms up!"

Jess grabbed a chunky mohair cardigan when they left. It kept the chill off her shoulders as they strode down the lane, and made her look more casual. She and Mathilde passed the harbour and the deli, the vintage clothing boutique, and the bookshop.

Rows of jaunty fairy lights and colourful Chinese lanterns festooned the outside of the Portlyon Folk Club and danced in the evening breeze. Cute, though Jessica, a really homey decoration. Rob must be getting engaged to someone very charming, no pretensions. She heard a cover of Van Morrison's 'Brown Ey'd Girl' from within.

Matty ordered them some drinks and Jess decided to adopt her usual post at parties, propping up the wall. Her aunt weaved her way through the crowd with two glasses of chilled chardonnay.

"Get your laughing gear around that!" She giggled at her niece and took a swig.

Jess sipped hers, "This isn't bad," she said approvingly.

"It's nice of you to say so," her aunt laughed, and spoke close to her ear so as to be heard over the music, "but we aren't savages!"

"Oh no, I didn't mean to be rude!"

"I know you didn't, my darling," and she winked at her. Matty rested her glass on a window ledge. "I'm off for a boogie. You coming?"

Jess shook her head, "Maybe later. I'll watch the drinks."

"Dorothy! You're not in Kansas anymore," Mathilde laughed again. "This is Cornwall not the West End. Safe here!" and she shimmied into the crowd and onto the makeshift wooden dancefloor.

Jess watched her go, thinking how different her life was going to be. Things had changed dramatically over the last few weeks. The red-faced partygoers danced in a carefree way. All together and unselfconscious. She compared their attitude to the average London bar. She took a deep breath and a swig of the good wine. She was happy to be a bystander.

A voice at her ear broke into her reverie and made her start.
Rob stood beside her. "I'm glad you could make it. You look – lovely."

Surprised and a little breathless she could not help but smile up at him. It was noisy around them, but she could look into his dark eyes. The covers band segued into Joni Mitchell's 'Big Yellow Taxi'. She thought about making conversation with him but could not think of anything to say. Instead she just nodded her thanks. All she really wanted to do was look at him, his eyes and the line of his jaw, now covered with an even dark stubble. She wanted to run her finger along it.

So, she took a deep breath, "What happened – with the lifeboat – yesterday?"
Rob held a pint of pale cider and leaned against the wooden pillar that stood behind her. She could only register his worn jeans that clung to his hips and the way the two top buttons were open at his collarbones. She could smell him again. He had a faintly salty, warm, musky scent. It worried her, enormously. She was at serious risk of doing something very inappropriate at his engagement party. Where was his fiancée? She should be watching him like a hawk.

"Bathers," he had to lean into her to be heard, "stranded by the tide. They took a dinghy out and got cut off."
She nodded, breathed deeply, but only caught his scent. She took a swig of wine. She noticed he was smiling at her. He coughed, shyly. "You look nice. Pretty." He took a drink too.

Jess searched the revellers for her aunt. Everyone there was dressed down, jeans and casual clothes.
"I think I'm a bit over-dressed for this," she admitted. "When you said it was an engagement party, I went for something smart."

20

"You look," he paused significantly whilst he searched for the words, "just lovely."

She had to do something, quickly, to break this spell.

"I haven't seen your fiancée yet. Fallon, did you say?"

He looked at her quizzically and then smiled. He laughed. "That's easily fixed," and he disappeared into the crowd.

Jess wanted the ground to open up and swallow her.

Within a minute he was back with a young woman by his side. His arm was around her shoulders affectionately. She was younger than he, shorter, and dressed in a denim shirt and drainpipe pastel pink jeans, frayed at the knees, with a pair of floral Dr. Marten patent lace-ups. Her hair was dark, like Rob's, and styled in a carefully cropped neat 1950s rockabilly quiff.

"Hello, I'm Fallon," she shook Jess's hand, a huge grin on her face and a pint of cider in her hand. "Thanks so much for coming. Rob tells me you've just moved into the Loft at the harbour."

"Hi, thanks for inviting me," Jess replied. "Yes, it was my father's home, he left it to me when he died. Congratulations on your engagement."

"I'm sorry – condolences."

"We weren't that close," Jess shook her head. "But I do miss him, yeah."

"Have you met my fiancée?" Fallon asked. Jess looked confused. "She's over there, dancing with your aunt."

Jess looked in the direction Fallon pointed. She saw a beautiful blonde woman dancing with Mathilde. She had a Dusty Springfield bouffant hair-do, geek girl specs, and wore a fitted blouse and a pencil skirt with stilettos that did not hinder her ability to dance in any way. Jess looked back at Rob who was grinning at her.

"Meet Fallon, my *sister*."

Jess smiled in return, with a sideways look at him.

"It's Cornwall," he laughed, "not the Dark Ages."

Fallon guessed at once, and detected the chemistry between them. "Has my big brother been winding you up? It's what he does best!"

Jess was grinning, then asked, "And when's the big day?"

"New Year's Eve," Fallon replied. "We know how to celebrate here." She looked closely at Jess, "So, you're Kris's daughter?"

21

Jess nodded.

"Kris," she smiled, "he was cool when I was a kid. Sorry for your loss." She looked at her brother, a silent signal passed between them, and back to Jess. "Enjoy," she patted him on the shoulder, "and don't take any garbage from this one!"

"All right, all right," he laughed. "Thank you, be on your way. Bye!" Jess waved as Fallon danced off with a cheeky smile.

Rob leaned in again, "Can I get you anything else?"
She shook her head, "I'm good, thanks." Why do I keep saying that? She asked herself. His face was close to hers. She conjured a different answer in her head, 'Yes, now that I know *you're* not getting married, you could give me a passionate kiss,' but she said nothing. Only smiled back.

His face was close to hers. The band started playing 'Eternal Flame' by The Bangles. Over Rob's shoulder she saw Lyla excitedly drag Fallon out onto the floor for a slow dance.

Rob's fingers gently brushed a tendril of stray hair from the side of Jessica's face. Her legs felt weak. He leaned in again, not to speak this time. She closed her eyes and his lips met hers.

It felt in that moment that her whole world shifted. His mouth was gentle at first, then insistent, and their tongues met and caressed. His hand moved to the back of her head. They parted briefly and he looked into her eyes. She knew she was flushed and her eyes were shining, that her feelings were on show, but she did not care. He looked down at her, his breathing came fast.

"Jessie," his voice was hoarse and they kissed again. She had not heard that childhood pet-name from anyone in years. She felt her groin catch fire. Seconds, minutes might have passed, she did not know or care. Time really did stand still.

"Close your eyes, give me your hand, darling. Do you feel my heart beating?" the singer did a great version of Suzanna Hoffs' vocals.

Rob's hand reached for hers and their fingers locked together. "Jessie," he breathed her name again.
"I think I need some air," she gasped. She turned to leave.

"I'll come with you," he held onto her hand and they threaded their way through the crowd. Out into the night air, Jess fled. Rob close behind. She reached the double doors onto the terrace of the club and burst outside.

'I'm thirty-one years of age,' she thought, 'I can't snog outside a club.'

She turned around and Rob was there. She almost fell into his arms. His hands found her waist and his mouth was on hers. Her head was spinning and it was not the wine. He kissed her deeply, holding her against this body. She thought, 'What the hell?' and melted into the strong arms of the lifeboat skipper. His touch was demanding, his hand kneaded the small of her back. She could hardly breathe. She felt overwhelmed. Ecstatic.

They parted, their breathing heavy, and looked into each other's eyes.

"I – I have to go," it took all her strength to tear herself away from him. She felt foggy and disoriented.

"No," he appealed, "I want you – to stay."

Jess rebelled, however. She stepped back from him. "I'm going," she insisted. And she turned on her heel and headed home.

5 FIRELIGHT

Jess lay on her bed in the studio. She stared up at the starlit autumn sky and calmed her pounding heart. This had been a crazy first three days in her new home.

She could still hear the music from the Folk Club drifting up the hill. She had left the club, past the other revellers. Shy, embarrassed, she threaded her way down the street. Everyone else was happy and relaxed. She wished she could be that way. And what an idiot she had been! She blushed again and rolled over onto her stomach, her face buried in the pillow. Kissing him like that.
"I've only been here five minutes," she groaned, "what will everyone think?"

And, she felt, more significantly, what will *he* think? I'm a little fool running off like that. Cinderella at midnight! Except, it's only nine-thirty, she looked up at the large factory clock that hung on one of the painted brick walls.

Well, no point in repeating my mistakes in my head. She got up and switched on the lamp and then drew the blinds. The large upper floor of the studio gave her room to breathe and decide how she felt. It gave her a wide view of the horizon and the elements through the generous windows but at night, with the blinds drawn, she felt alone, like a ship on a sea, lost in her own world. Mostly alone, throughout her life, she did not mind and was ready to face the future. She still felt wired from the evening's activity and not yet ready for sleep. She changed into a pair of scruffy jeans and a t-shirt. So silly, she thought again, to dress up like that for a drink in the local club.
"What was I thinking?"

24

This question was still going around in her head as she went downstairs to the ground floor of the Sailmaker's Loft. This had been Kristof's living space. A curtained-off bed and a couple of distressed, over-stuffed sofas reminded her of her holidays. She and her father had spent many an evening in front of the wood-burner playing Scrabble and Boggle. Her father had loved one-on-one time with word games. He had been very competitive and never gave her an easy win.

Jess flicked on a lamp and she was met with the glorious view of the posters for Cornish holidays, designed by Kristof. Colour blocks of sky and sea were punctuated with striped deck chairs and white seabirds. He had used some of his mass-produced print designs to paper the walls of his downstairs den. She began to tidy the surfaces and cupboards of the detritus left from moving in, and from her father's leftover life. Magazines, old envelopes, shopping lists, and invoices from art suppliers. She knew there would be nothing beyond this mundane, workaday evidence of his life. Nothing personal was left, no drawings or examples of his handwriting. Nothing direct from Kristof. Third wife, Maxine, had seen to that. She managed everything for him and saw to it that anything of value was transferred to their house in France. Maxine went through every inch of the Loft. The posters that papered the walls were the only really personal touch left by him. She could not remove them without damage. And they were prints and not originals. So, she left them.

Jess worked her way through shelves and boxes. She tied a bandana around her head as the dust rose. Worn wood, tongue and groove panels with crackled and blistered paint, sturdy stone walls. When she surveyed everything after she cleared the clutter she realised that there was plenty of floor space, along with the generous fireplace that housed the wood-burner. A set of folding tables and chairs stood in one corner. She lifted them out and started to arrange them into a seating plan. Restaurant sections. Only six tables, but they were sturdy, metal, with a painted enamel coating. Their origins were probably from some long-forgotten party thrown by Kristof, on a whim. She lit a fire in the stove.

Jess stood back and looked at the set-up of small intimate tables. In her imagination she pictured a brunch and supper room, with a barista bar in one corner, perhaps? Could she do it? Could she run her own little business, here, working on what she loved? Fresh ingredients from local suppliers. She was right beside the harbour, for heaven's sake, on site for fresh fish. And then her mind raced back to Rob again. She smiled and shook her head.

A knock at the door.

"Coming," she called out. That must be Mathilde, she thought. I left her at the club with no explanation. She drew aside the curtain and opened the door, saying, "I'm so sorry, Aunty, I remembered I had something to do."
But it was not her Aunty.

Rob Tredegar's tall figure filled the doorway. He had one hand raised to lean against the frame. A rush of cool night air reached her, making her skin tingle. She gaped a little in surprise. He smiled. Dark stubble on his chin and his strong arms were revealed by rolled up sleeves. He stood casually, one hand in his jeans' pocket. His head was tilted to one side and he smiled.
"Your aunty asked if I would check on you."
Jess swallowed, "She must be worried, I should go back."
"It's ok, she said to just text her. She's having fun and didn't want to leave."
"Ok," Jess paused. "I didn't mean to leave like that. I did remember that I've got things to do."
He walked in.

"The fire's lit. I'll text my aunt." Jess surprised herself at how cool she could be. It was his turn to be nervous. She sent the text off and then shook out a mohair blanket. She laid it across one of the sofas and invited him to sit down.

"I don't have any cider," she noticed how he ran his hand through his thick hair as he sat, "but there is some red wine – a very good bottle – in one of the boxes. It was a farewell gift from work."

"Red's great. I like red wine. Great," he nodded and tried to relax on the baggy sofa. "Work – what did you do in London?"

"I'm a chef," she unsealed the top of the bottle of wine and retrieved a corkscrew. She handed both to him. "Will you do the honours?"

"Sure," he took them from her but seemed a little confused. As she found some tumblers he said, "I have a confession to make."

"What's that?"

"Well, two actually."

She brought the glasses over.

"First," he was trying to figure out the corkscrew, it was an expensive lever-style one, "your aunt didn't ask me to come and check on you. I offered – to make sure I hadn't upset you."

"I'm not upset," and she took the bottle and corkscrew from him. With expert restaurant-experienced hands she twisted it into the top of the bottle. "And what else do you have to confess to?"

He looked down at his work boots.

"I think I might have offended you the other night. We were joking around when we brought the catch in. But I realised that you might have thought we were laughing at you. We weren't – I would never -," he added quickly.

"That's ok," she felt more relieved than she thought she would. She pulled at the corkscrew but it was stuck tight.

"Here," he offered, "let me. That I *can* do. Anything that requires brute force and ignorance." They both laughed.

"It's a sign of a good bottle, a tough cork."

"Really?" he looked interested.

"No," she giggled, "I don't know!"

"You got me!" He held the bottle firmly, gripping it, and she watched him draw the cork with a loud 'Pop!'

Jess watched the muscles in his arms stiffen and then relax. He took one of the glasses and was about to pour when she put her hand on his arm, "Let it breathe," she sat down on the sofa and he joined her. They both relaxed a little.

"Breathe, right," he nodded again and knitted his fingers together. "So … you're a chef?"

"Hmmm," she nodded too. "And you're a fisherman *and* a lifeboatman?"

He laughed, in a relaxed way, "How do you do? My name is Robert, and you must be Jessica?" he gave her a firm handshake.

"You do have a good handshake, my father must have liked you."

"I don't know about that, but he certainly put me to work. I must have been the last person to fix up the fireplace. I repointed the mortar between the stones."

"So, you have quite a history with this place?"

They talked about her work. He was interested in her travels, how she had toured Europe and Asia, learning her craft. Fashionable restaurants were open to her because she was Kristof Trelawny's daughter, but she chose instead to work at a family bistro near her mother's flat in West London. Giovanni and Maria had run their business for nearly forty years, so she figured they had been doing something right all that time.

"They were great teachers, and we had a lot of laughs."

After that grounding she had worked her way up to running a brigade.

"Will you cook for me?"

"You're very forward, aren't you? I'm a Londoner, I'm not used to this familiarity!"

"You're no Londoner, you're a Trelawny!" and he moved closer to her.

She found herself getting a little nervous again.

"I like to hear your laugh," he said quietly.

She allowed him into her personal space. She felt more confident now, powerful and in control of their encounter. It was a mutual impulse between them, but calmer this time. His hand reached for hers. His dark eyes intensely scrutinised her pale lilac eyes. She smiled slightly and moved towards him. Rob's hand stroked the side of her face and then they moved into one another, naturally, eagerly, and kissed. Deep, passionate, their breathing quickened. Jess felt her blood surge. Her heart thumped. His tongue parted her lips and darted into her mouth. Her hands moved up to his hair and she caught his smooth, dark curls, twisting her fingers into them. His hand reached for her waist. They parted for a second to catch their breath and their eyes locked together. He kissed her again, quickly, passionately and pulled her into an embrace, "Oh, Jessie, Jessie!"

She grew bolder, throwing all caution aside, with intense arousal mounting in her. "We must be crazy," she breathed as he kissed her neck, "we hardly know each other! What's you surname, again?"
"It's Tredegar," he kissed her between his words, "Rob Tredegar."
She looked at his gorgeous face, they smiled at each other. His hand moved down her back, she moved closer to him and slid her hands inside the neck of his shirt.
Naturally, easily she moved to sit astride him on the sofa before the fire. His face was level with her breasts and he kissed and fondled them through the fabric of her shirt. She could feel his need for her and she longed to satisfy herself. She undid her shirt and saw the dark lust in his eyes as he looked at her full breasts held by her smooth cotton bra. The intense pleasure they both felt threatened to overwhelm them.
"I didn't wear the fancy one," she laughed breathlessly, "but I don't think that matters, does it?"
He smiled up at her as his hands and mouth explored her body.

So far, they had not removed any clothing fully, but their bodies were in perfect harmony with a natural passion that made nothing else matter. He kissed her and breathed her name. This made her hips arch towards him. She had never felt so certain of anything in her life up to this moment. Jess moved off him slightly and he shifted over so they could unbutton and unzip clothing. She started to giggle.
"Are you ok?" Rob smiled breathlessly.
"Oh yes!" she kissed him again. She knew she wanted him so much and with such happiness it made her feel giddy.
Rob unbelted his jeans.

A shrill beeping disturbed them. For a moment they both froze. Jess, confused, looked around.

29

"My pager!" Rob grabbed for it. "I've got to go!"
He looked completely desolate. He leapt over the back of the sofa and did his trousers up, slightly hunched over thanks to his arousal. He belted them carefully. He looked at her with a pleading expression on his face, "Rain check? You'll be here when I get back?" and gave her a quick, earnest, kiss on the lips.
Jess knelt on the sofa, her shirt modestly held against her breasts, and she nodded, wordless.

Rob headed for the door, and she was able to stammer out, "Be – be careful!"
He paused on the threshold and gave her his joker's smile, "I'm *always* careful." And then he was out into the night and gone.
Jess looked at the door and the darkness beyond. With a heavy groan she threw herself on the sofa.

She looked at the open bottle of wine on the table.

6 SECOND THOUGHTS

Jess woke early. The fire in the wood-burner was grey and dry. She felt chilly, and a little fuzzy. She pulled the mohair blanket around her and then her eyes flashed open. 'Rob!' she remembered with a start. He was on his 'shout'. She flipped the blanket off and leaped up. Then she thought for a moment and smiled at the 'rain check'.

Soon, she was happily cooking. She prepared a packed breakfast; some spicy sausages on crusty bread, griddled eggs with paprika, sandwiched together with her own recipe aioli and a sprinkle of fresh, chopped coriander. She wrapped everything into a brown paper parcel. The ultimate breakfast sandwich. It's what the skipper of a lifeboat deserved after a night out on a rescue, she figured. With a flask of freshly ground coffee, what more could he ask for? Except, she thought, perhaps me?

Jess even spruced herself up in the mirror. She tried to do her hair, gave up, and put on fresh linen shorts and a Breton top. Feeling pleased with her jaunty look she pulled on worn sneakers and tied a perky bandana in her hair. She applied a little lip gloss and teased a few curls around her cheeks.

She trotted down the wooden stairs to the breezy quayside as the lifeboat came in and stood at a distance to watch the crew of four set about mooring the boat. Rob the coxswain, in waterproofs and in charge, organised his fellow crew. They all looked tired. He was handsome and exhausted.

31

From her vantage point she could watch him in action.

"Morning," a voice beside her spoke politely. "You've just moved into the Loft, am I right?"

"Yes," Jess turned and smiled to the elderly gentleman who stood beside her now, with his elderly grey-haired terrier who stood beside him with crooked little legs.

"Simon – Simon Evans," he held out a hand to her.

She shook it, "Jessica Trelawny."

"Oh, I know you – as I am sure most folk around here have been saying! I remember your father. I run the second-hand bookshop in the High Street."

He gestured towards the lifeboat, "Bad business this, last night. Two pleasure craft in trouble. Tourists and part-time sailors think they can navigate as far as Bristol. They underestimate the autumn weather. Just because it's sunny on land. They didn't check the forecast – children aboard. That's always the hardest."

With this information, Jess realised just what a sacrifice Rob and his crew made every time they went out. Other people's folly and over-confidence meant they must risk their lives regularly.

She chatted to Simon, listened to his reminiscences about her father and her summers. She did not notice the other people on the quay for a few minutes. When she did look round she saw a tall, attractive woman who ran forward enthusiastically just as Rob disembarked. She threw her arms around his neck and kissed him.

Jess had been going to step forward with her perfect breakfast parcel but she halted in her tracks. The woman kissed Rob in a familiar, possessive way. He had his back to Jess. She saw his arms circle the woman's waist briefly and he laughed then held her away from him whilst she looked lovingly into his eyes. They did not notice her. She felt stupid, embarrassed. She knew she had to get clear before they saw her. On an impulse, she turned to Simon with the breakfast sandwich.

"Please, have this," and she handed it to him, "I made too much."

A little surprised, he thanked her as she walked quickly away.

32

She headed back to the Loft. She wanted to put aside all the messy feelings, shove them out of her head. 'What a silly, silly fool I am,' she thought as she strode away from the harbour, her cheeks hot, 'what an idiot!'

Once inside, she put on some work overalls and began to scrub out the kitchenette. She decided to prepare everything for decorating. She threw herself into this task, and began to formulate a plan after a little while. She would clean down the space and get it renovated as soon as possible for an opening. An opening of a new restaurant – *her* restaurant and business. She had capital, she had premises, she could do this.

As she worked away at the surfaces with a bucket of soapy water and some sugar soap on the brick and old plaster, there was a knock at the studio door.

Rob stood outside.

He looked tired. He had obviously come over immediately after the boat had been docked and equipment stowed, to be with her. That is, after his fond reunion with the attractive, eager woman.

Jess opened the door to him, and he stepped towards her, instinctively, with his arms held out. To continue where he left off, evidently. She stepped back. He paused.
"Jessie?" he looked a little confused. "I came back as soon as I could," he laughed. "You can't blame me for leaving, it wasn't my fault." He saw the hurt expression in her eyes and stopped talking. He reached for her hand, kindly.
I could fall, she realised, for all this – for this act of his. She moved further away to avoid his touch, as if scalded by hot water.
"What's wrong?"
"Nothing – nothing's wrong with me. Now."
"What? What did I do, or not do? I know you don't blame me for having to leave!"

"No. I'm just trying to say that it gave me a chance to think about things and I realised I was making a mistake. I had been drinking and I don't want to start anything. I can't get involved."

"I don't get it," he looked confused, "what's changed?"

She walked away from him. Casually. She wanted to sound unconcerned and unhurt.

"I am trying to start a new life here. I want to open a new business. I don't need any complications or distractions." She hoped he might explain himself. She did not say anything else, perhaps he would fill the silence.

Rob looked at her steadily, with a frown, and after a pause he said, "Well, at least you admit I distract you."

She watched him leave.
He did not look back, not once.

Jess unsealed a paint pot and grabbed a brush.

7 SALVAGED

"I found these in my airing cupboard."
Mathilde bustled into the Loft.

"There are some beautiful prints amongst them, a little worn, but with a vintage look. They might do for something." She laid out a pile of decorative fabrics, each one with a quaint or classic pattern. "Can you use them?"
Jess put down her sanding block and came to check them out.

Over the past two weeks, since she had moved to Portlyon, she had made great progress with the Sailmaker's Loft renovations. The upstairs was now her living space with a new bank of stainless-steel kitchen worktops, a large oven, and a range along one wall. She had a scaled-down professional kitchen, a version of what she was used to in a large restaurant, fitted into the Loft ready to service the charming downstairs dining room. This space, she had begun to fit out in an eclectic and thoughtful fashion. In and out of the roof beams she strung some simple, white lights. They danced above the mis-matched chairs and tables, each one of which a little work of art in its own right. Some she had salvaged, some had been donated. Jess and Lyla painted each in a distinctive style, with stencilled decoration. The flagstones underfoot had been polished and a new set of rugs laid down.

As yet, she did not know what to do with the bare stone walls. So, for the time being she had draped some coloured fabrics around the room and from the beams, stretched across the uneven surfaces. Her father's posters held pride of place on one wall and drew the eye. It looked good so far, but there was much left to do. The next task was to get a carpenter in, and a builder, to have some serious construction work done. But these things could wait. First, she wanted to test her market and have a soft opening for the restaurant as soon as she could. She wanted to create an evening with a tasting menu for patrons to pay what they felt was deserved.

Lost in thought, Jess drew her aunt's attention. Mathilde placed a hand on her shoulder.
"Are you all right, my love? You seem sad lately. What's wrong?"
"Nothing," Jess smiled, thinking how she needed to get something like a normal, cheerful expression on her face. She had tried to create a new routine. She had not seen Rob since that morning, except from a distance. "I'm fine. I just want to get everything fixed up." She gave what she thought was a casual smile to reassure her aunt.
"Well then, we'll have to think about what the menu will offer. When do you think you'll be open?"
"Two weeks from today. That will give me time to finish preparing. I can source and order ingredients from local suppliers. I won't go far afield. Low mileage menu."
"That sounds – progressive!" Matty laughed.
"I'm going out today to try some foraging for ingredients. See if I can find anything useful."
"Forage? For ingredients? How peculiar!"
"It's not so strange these days, Aunty. There are lots of resources out there and flavours to be had. Things that grow wild – they're free and I can make use of them."

Later that morning, Jess took her basket and walked out to the clifftop. Mathilde, immensely curious, went with her.
"I'm sure we'll find something if we look down here. There could be sea aster or some wild samphire."
"Very well," Matty was still a little doubtful, "lead on."

They walked along the clifftop path and scoured the area. Jess looked down at the sheer rocks to Penlyon Cove. Nothing could be seen from above, however, so she decided on a new plan. "Let's go down to the shoreline," she said. "I think we can get a better view from below up to the cliffs, there."

The two made their way carefully down the stairway cut into the wall of the cove. Some autumn drizzle fell as they walked along the shore. Jess scanned the sands and the shingle, the rocks and pools, as well as the cliff wall above them. Matty looked up at the layered Cornish stone. To her eyes there was nothing there worth harvesting, or foraging, as her niece insisted. Jess, in the meantime, had started to scramble up the cliffs. She had spotted something about twenty feet above the beach. On a ledge, she could perch and just reach up towards what looked like some wild samphire plants. These were the best subtle little native succulents that clung to stony cliffs and offered a peppery, juicy flavour to fish dishes. The details were important in the restaurant business.

Mathilde called up to her, "Be careful, darling, I don't think that's stable."
Jess craned across the cliff face towards the greenery.
"No, it's ok. I can just reach it."
Her basket dropped and bounced down the rocks.

"Watch out!" Mathilde was instantly afraid. "Oh, come down, please come down, do!"
"I can reach it," Jess held on to another ledge to steady herself.
A flurry of stones clattered and she slipped. Skidding down part of the slope, she was at once filled with a lurching terror. Her foot lodged in a gap and her ankle twisted. Pain shot through her and she scrambled to hold on. She found a hold to cling onto and whilst her ankle throbbed she looked up and down the cliff. She realised she could neither climb up or down. For the time being, all she could do was hold on where she was.

Matty cried out during all of this, "Stay there, don't move. I'll call for help."
She took out her phone, and in a fluster called the emergency services. "It's Portlyon – the cove – Penlyon Cove. Hurry, hurry!"

37

Jess fleetingly felt she ought to tell her not to call anyone and she could manage to climb down on her own. But when she moved her foot the cliff face crumbled and she looked around to realise there really was no way up or down.

"Hang on," Mathilde advised again, "it's too unstable, it won't hold you."

Jess looked down and then up, and resolved to hang on.

"I'm through to the coastguard now," her aunt called out, "they are going to send someone. Hang on. Oh, please hang on!"

Jess stabilised herself as best she could on the ledge. If she moved she sent a tumble of rock debris down the cliff. So, she took a deep breath and awaited her rescue.

Time passed. It seemed like an age. Matty called out reassuring things to her throughout the wait. Eventually, she heard sirens on the clifftop above.

"Oh, they're coming, they're coming. Hang on, darling!"

"I *am* hanging on!"

She became aware of some activity above her. Pebbles scattered down, so she hid her face against her arm and closed her eyes. She heard and felt someone drop down next to her.

A familiar voice spoke beside her, "It's all right, I've got you now."

Jess looked up into Rob's kind, handsome face. This time he wore a concerned, serious expression, reassuring and comforting. He was suspended by a set of lines and wore a harness and safety helmet.

"Are you ok?"

She nodded and managed a quiet, "Yes."

"We'll have you back on level ground in no time." He used his professional manner, in work mode as a rescuer. "Are you hurt?" he asked as he put a safety helmet on her head.

"It's just my ankle. It's quite painful."

"Well, we'll get the weight off it soon."

Rob smiled as he looped another harness around her so that she was attached to him.

"Put your arms around me," he spoke softly and with authority, their faces close together. Jess felt her cheeks flushing deeply. She hoped he would not notice. He clipped her harness to the lines that held him.

"Now, they'll haul us up. You're not afraid, are you?"

She held onto him, feeling the tension in his muscles, and shook her head. She tried her best to avoid eye contact as they were hauled up the rock face. His breathing was steady. Every time the rope tensed they were raised a little further towards the top. A portable gantry was in place that fed the rope out, with two more members of the rescue team to assist.

Jess was locked against him. As close as they had been on that first night. He was pressed to her and she had to hold him tightly. The attempt to avoid eye contact was working until she looked down at the beach and immediately felt dizzy. The sharp rocks fell away to the shingle below, with Matty a small figure looking upwards, anxiously shielding her eyes from the bright, drizzly sky. Rob sensed her discomfort and spoke reassuringly.

"Don't look down, fix your eyes on me."

Cautiously, she looked at him. At once she felt better. He felt her arms relax. He fixed his gaze on her and smiled. Not a joking smile, but one full of warmth and concern. "That's it. Just relax. It will soon be over."

His cheek was close to hers. She could feel his breath. Her arms wrapped around him and she gripped the solid strength of his back. Her insides fluttered.

Suddenly, she realised how much she did not want this to be over. She did not want to leave his side and be released from the safety and comfort of his warm strength. But she had to shake off these stupefying feelings. This was neither the time nor the place to have them.

Once at the top, competent hands reached for her and she was unhitched from the harness. Jess was passed from the safety of Rob's arms and as soon as she put her foot on the ground she winced in pain and her ankle buckled underneath her. Both grateful and embarrassed she was put in the back of the waiting ambulance. A paramedic gently manipulated her ankle and asked, "Does this hurt? Or this?"

Distracted, she looked across to where Rob was winding up the ropes and loading the back of the rescue Landrover. He was casual and business-like with his two colleagues. She took the chance to take in the sight of him – from head to toe – as she mechanically answered the paramedic's questions.

Rob shared a laugh and a joke, the familiar smile, relaxed now the job was finished. She got it now, she understood him better. She was still looking at him from the rear of the ambulance when he turned around and caught her eye just before the medic shut the doors. A smile full of warmth and kindness creased his face. She felt her heart ache.

Why did he have to be like this? One minute he was charming, reliable, brave, and the next he turned out to be cheating on someone. She felt both intensely grateful to him and deeply hurt. Just as the ambulance started to pull away she realised she had not even thanked him.

8 BONDED

"I've put together a basket of essential oils. Alastair is on his way as of ten o'clock this morning. I can't believe that you and your Aunt were out being so foolish. Is she there?"
Lizbeth was on speaker phone. Jess and Matty were in the Loft.

Jess's foot was in a 'walking' boot brace for her torn ligaments. Matty had a large pot of tea ready.
"Mum, it's really not necessary to send Alastair all the way down here like that. This is Cornwall, I can find essential oils!"
"Not the kind of quality you need. You don't want some quack concocting any old rubbish for you. These are bespoke, from my aromatherapy healer at Camden Lock. Is Mathilde there?"
"Yes, Lizbeth, I'm here. It's so lovely to hear your voice!"
The aunt grinned at her niece.
"What were you thinking? I can't believe you let her fall off a cliff! She could have been killed!"
"I didn't *let* her, Lizbeth. She was climbing up to pick some --,"
"And she could have died. I knew I shouldn't have entrusted my only child to you!"

Matty looked at Jess and raised her hands in a gesture of helplessness.
Jess mouthed, 'I'm sorry,' and shook her head.
"Mother," she picked up the phone, "you're breaking up, the coverage is lousy here. Speak soon!"
"Alastair will be there by seven or so. Oh darling, take care!"
Jessica hung up the call and sighed, "Please, don't take what she says too seriously."

"My dear, I never do. Lizbeth and I go way back."

There was a tap at the door.

"I'll get it," Matty bustled over.

Jess stood and hobbled, balancing on the walking boot so she could navigate the room. At the door, Fallon and Lyla stood smiling, bearing flowers and a gift basket of cookies and muffins.

"Can we come in?" Lyla peeped in around Matty and gasped, "Oh my word!" when she saw Jess. She rushed forwards to hug her.

"How are you feeling?" Fallon was more restrained.

"Matty told us what happened, you're so brave." Lyla deposited the flowers and gifts on the table.

"I'm ok, really. They didn't even keep me in overnight. It's torn ligaments, not a break thankfully."

"How long will it take to heal?" Fallon and Lyla accepted a cup of tea from Matty and settled in for a visit.

"About two months," she sighed. "It's going to mess with my schedule for the restaurant." Then she recalled, "By the way, please thank your brother for me. I wasn't able to do it myself. The ambulance whisked me away."

Fallon brushed it off, "Don't worry, it's what he does – that's the way he is. But I'll get him to drop by so you can thank him in person. Not that he needs to get any more attention. His head won't fit through the door as it is."

"Is he really like that? Arrogant?"

"Not at all," Matty cut in, "he's wonderful!"

"Please!" Fallon laughed. "He's fine. He's just my big brother."

"Never mind Rob," Lyla came and sat next to Jess. As Fallon's fiancée spoke to her, Jess could not help but let her thoughts stray towards Rob and if he might come over.

Lyla was talking to her, "And, as you know, our celebration is on New Year's Eve. We want to have a really special event."

"Of course," Jess came back to the conversation.

"So," Lyla grasped her hand and looked at Fallon, grinning, "We both wondered if we could book this place for our wedding party? We'll be at the town hall for the vows and then we want to have our

reception here – if you could cater it?" She blurted out before Jess could reply, "Say yes, say yes, please say yes!"
Fallon interrupted her, "Give her a chance to speak. What are you, twelve?"

Jess looked at both of them, "I don't have anything ready here! I had hoped that the soft opening could go ahead two weeks from now, but with this," she looked at her leg.
Mathilde stood up, "That's why we'll stage an intervention!" she declared. "Let's get everyone we know who can spare the time to work on the opening so that you can be up and running and you'll be able to host the reception here by New Year. If we all pitch in we can get you started."
"Yes," Lyla agreed. "Let us help. If we all do a little bit whilst you are laid up then it'll spread the load and when you're better you can take it on from there. It's going to be worth our while."
"I'll be wearing this for at least another month. It's too much to ask of you."
"Nonsense," Matty cleared away the tea things. "You're my family, and these are my friends and neighbours. We'll rally round to help you out."

Lyla and Fallon stood up to leave.
"We'll be back tomorrow, and we'll get you some more supplies, and then we can start the work as soon as possible. Rob will do the heavy stuff." Lyla hugged Jess, who could only feel nervous about the idea. "And thank you, thank you. This will be my dream venue for the reception."
"Come on, she's got to get her rest," and Matty helped Jess plump some pillows to put her foot up.

Jess must have slept for a couple of hours after that. She awoke and the air in the Loft felt chilly but she stretched in the warm comfort of the bed under a fleece blanket. The painkillers were certainly hitting the spot, she thought. She hopped up and hobbled to the bathroom, turned on the shower and brushed her teeth. A little while later, she was busy rinsing her hair with her booted leg outside the shower curtain, when she heard a noise outside in the Loft. She limped out of the cubicle and grabbed her robe then slid the door of the shower room open.

"Who's there?"

In the evening sunlight that flooded the Loft, Rob stood. A large box of groceries in his arms.

The two looked at each other. Her hair wet from the shower, the flimsy robe wrapped around her. She saw his eyes flicker down her body and quickly back up again.

"I'm, I'm so sorry," he stammered, and looked away. "I'll just leave these here." He placed the box on the counter. "I knocked, but there was no answer. Your Aunt and my sister asked me to bring you some supplies. They couldn't wait."

She relaxed a little.

"That's ok, thank you."

"I thought that if I just nipped inside with them I wouldn't have to bother you. I didn't want to leave them outside."

"You're not bothering me."

"You might not have had to see me."

Jess felt flustered and awkward again.

"I'll leave you alone."

"No, wait," she limped forwards, "you mustn't run off – I can't move very fast." She steadied herself against the kitchen counter. Rob stopped and turned his head to her, then he grinned. She needed the support of the counter right then, as she felt herself go weak.

"I want to thank you," she said quietly. "Thank you, and your crew for getting me up safely."

"It was a pleasure," he stayed near the door, not wishing to overstep the mark or outstay his welcome, but neither did he seem to want to leave.

Jess hobbled around the kitchen counter and attempted to limp across to the window seat. Rob moved quickly to her and took an arm before she could object, and helped her to sit.

"Let me get you a stool."

"There's really no need."

"Your aunt and my sister would wring my neck if something else happened to you."

"I think I'm safe with you!" she laughed, and then realised that sounded more loaded than she had meant it too. "Thank you," when he put a cushion behind her, and she happily rested. She noticed that her robe had slipped from her shoulder. She shyly raised it.

"Can I do – anything?" he asked, trying his best not to look down, keeping his eyes on her face.

"You can sit here for a bit, if you like?"

"Yes, I'd like that."

They sat in silence for a little, embarrassed.

Jess spoke, "How long have you -," she had interrupted him.

"So, you were up there picking - ," he had interrupted her.

They laughed.

"Ten years, crewing, and two years as coxswain."

"Wild samphire, it goes well with fish."

It was difficult to be in his company and feel anything but happy.

A knock at the door. It was Alastair. Rob leapt up to let him in. Jess felt relief.

He too, carried a box.

"Hello, looks like I'm not the only one that's brought supplies. I come bearing gifts, from your Mother." Alastair nodded to Rob, "Thanks, son."

"Alastair, this is Rob. Rob, Alastair. Rob is my rescuer. He brought me back up the cliff."

"So, it's you we have to thank! Good man."

He deposited the box on the counter. It happened to be a crate from a very elegant London grocer. Jess hobbled over and investigated it.

"Figs, rosemary syrup, and so many cheeses!"

"*And* there's a crate of ales and wines in the van."

"In that case, dinner is on me," she announced. "If you can come all this way with the ingredients, the least I can do is cook them for you.

And it will give me a chance to thank you properly," she smiled at Rob.

"You mustn't go to any trouble," Rob's face, full of hope, contradicted his words.

Jess decided to risk it. The best of both worlds, Alastair's presence would prevent anything happening with Rob, but at least she could get him to stay.

"You'd not refuse the offer, young Rob, if you'd tasted her cooking."

"I haven't yet had the pleasure," he looked right at Jess.

"It's no trouble," she said quickly – "what's the fresh catch today?" she smiled.

"I think I can find something for your table," and he headed for the door, "got any samphire?" and he winked, then was off at a pace, whilst she smiled at him.

"He seems like a good 'un," Alastair observed, "is he always in such a hurry?"

Smiling and warm, laughing and talking, Jess cooked fresh herring with lemon and herb butter, followed by roasted figs cooked in brandy with rosemary syrup. Alastair and Rob made a dent in some of the bottles of craft ale. Jess went without booze thanks to her strong painkillers, but she more than enjoyed watching the two men bond.

They sat until Alastair yawned widely.

"You can have the sofa downstairs again, Al."

"Not me, girl," he stretched again, "these old bones can't handle another night on that thing. I'm booked into a B&B down the road. I'll say goodnight to you – and you. No, I'll see myself out," and he got up to go. "I'll see you in the morning. I have my orders from your mother and your aunt, to help get the place all fixed up." He moved around the table and kissed her on the top of the head.

Jess squeezed his hand, "Thank you, this all means so much to me."

After he had left, Jess started to clear the table. Rob stood immediately, "Please, let me." His hand, accidentally it seemed, rested on hers.

She moved it away at once, as if she had been scalded. "No, I'll do it." She hobbled over to the sink. He stood alone by the table and ran his hand through his hair.

"Jessie," he followed her. She turned to face him. Now he was close to her and she knew she could not trust herself. "Jessie," he spoke her pet-name again and fondled one of her messy curls. She looked up at him, and leaned ever so slightly towards him.

The feelings were happening again. She grew certain. More certain than anything else in the world. If everything else was taken away and he remained, that would be enough.

Cautiously, he looked down at her and gently kissed her mouth. When she responded, he grew more eager. His hand moved around her waist. He pushed his tongue into her mouth, gently exploring, and she responded again. She had to use the countertop to support herself, until she put her arms around his neck. Then he held her up. They parted slightly.

"Are you ok?" his eyes searched her face.

She nodded, breathing hard.

"Oh, Jessie, I want you so much I can scarcely breathe." He searched her face again, his lips brushed hers gently. "Will you – do you want to?"

She held his face in her hands and kissed him clearly and strongly. He tasted of the rich, warm ale, and a gentle note of rosemary.

"Yes," she smiled, "I want you."

9 HARMONY

Breathing hard, Rob and Jess continued to kiss one another passionately. Night surrounded them in the Loft.

She paused, and looked down at the boot on her injured leg.
"I'm going to need some help?" she smiled, embarrassed. He returned her smile, free and relaxed. She felt he looked like a man who had just received everything he had ever wanted.
"It's ok, I've got you," and he swept her up in his arms.
She was stunned at the ease with which he carried her to the bed and laid her down, carefully, gently. They kissed again. She could not get enough of his lips. She held him as he settled beside her, avoiding her leg. She felt the powerful ache for him.
He paused again, "Are you sure this is what you want?"
She nodded, dumbly, and they kissed again, hard. His tongue was against hers. They sucked and strained on each other's mouths. His hand raked down her body to her hips. She reached for him as the softness of his mouth enveloped hers and she laid one hand on her breast.
"It's ok," she murmured, "touch me, I want you, I do want you. You don't have to be too gentle."

Yes, she decided, I do want him, more than anything. I'll be the 'other' woman. If this is my fate, as it must be, like my mother. I've fallen for someone just like she did for my father. He'll give me his temporary self and then go back to her, or on to the next woman.

Rob whispered her name, kissed her neck softly and tenderly, stroked her breast, isolating the nipple through her clothes. Her back

48

arched and she shuddered. He pulled back, and laughed softly, "I'm going to have to use that move again."

"Please do!" and her hands explored his body with abandon. She slipped them into his shirt and felt his warm, muscular body as they melted into one another. She dug her nails into his shoulder.

Rob winced and laughed. He looked down at her and arched a dark eyebrow, "Oh yes?"

He raised up and knelt on the bed, and started to try and pull his shirt off. The cuffs were buttoned, so he pulled and pulled. Buttons pinged off and flew around the room.

He lay along her body and began to undress her. His hard, strong, tanned body, against her pale, blonde flesh. Jess reached down to his hips and felt his desire. She ached for him, to her core. He responded, somewhat startled, and looked at her for reassurance. She sat up awkwardly because of her leg, feeling flushed and clumsy. "I think I'll need some help."

"I'll take care of it."

In his eagerness to shed his trousers at the side of the bed he nearly fell over. They both laughed.

Night had closed in, surrounding the Loft. Stars could be seen through the skylight. He stood in his loose boxer shorts and rapidly drew the blinds near the bed. A chill had started to settle in the room, but that had no effect on his desire, she could see. He shivered exaggeratedly and snuggled down beside her in the bed, pulling a fleece blanket over the both of them.

Kissing her, Rob peeled off her t-shirt and undid the clasp of her bra. He paused when he saw her soft, naked breasts. His eyes were dark with lust as he kissed first one, then the other, teasing her nipples with his tongue and teeth. She gasped again and again, without thinking, without reasoning now. It had to happen. She had on a pair of her usual denim shorts. He wriggled them down, slowly now. He savoured the closeness to her flesh this gave him, and grazed his mouth along her thigh. His strong fingers edged the shorts carefully over her strapped up ankle.

"You can just lie still, I'll do everything," he spoke softly, his voice low with passion, as he slipped off his underwear.

She took in the sight of his body, firm torso, muscular arms that she had longed for that first night. She felt overwhelmed with desire for him, but also shy about her imperfections. She was not tall or long-limbed. But he did not notice anything that she considered her flaws. He gazed at her body, "Jessie, you are so beautiful," he whispered as he focused on her mouth, her breasts, hips, and being as close to her as possible. He eased down her panties and cast them to one side. She looked at him, looking down at her.

Rob kissed her body over and over, in the soft light of the lamp by the studio bed. She knitted her fingers in his tousled dark hair. She could feel his breath against her flesh, she was on fire. He began to kiss her mound and she arched towards him. His fingers found her clitoris and massaged it gently. She began to shudder and spasm. His tongue was working her now and his fingers dipped inside her. She began to feel her climax building. Her hand reached out to the side of the bed, where his trousers rested. She felt a small square, plastic object under her fingers.
"Wait," her hand stilled the back of his head. He stopped what he was doing immediately.
"What – what is it? Am I doing it wrong?"
"No, no – not at all!" she gasped. "It's this," she picked up his RNLI rescue alert pager. "Is there any way we can shut this thing off? I'm being *really* selfish, I know."
He laughed and kissed her. She tasted herself on his mouth.
"It's ok, I'm not on call tonight."
"Thank goodness," she sighed with huge relief. "I don't feel like sharing you tonight."
"You have my full attention."

Afterwards, they lay together. The powerful, sweeping orgasms she had enjoyed with him were something she secretly marvelled at. They both felt how well they fit together. Their bodies worked in harmony. He had cried out how beautiful she was when he finally orgasmed, and lain into her neck, kissing her softly. She had felt like crying. She had to banish the feelings of sadness that threatened to overwhelm her. This would be the one and only time she could be like this with him. She would have to back away from anything else, send him back to her. For now, though, she savoured the closeness and the creation of a perfect memory of one night with him. They did fit together, so well. And that fact made her feel even more sad.

Rob had not finished. He made love to her again and she urged him, "You don't have to be gentle." He came hard inside her, holding her tight and gasping. His handsome face contorted into a look of extreme pleasure.

"Jessie, Jessie," he breathed her name as their hearts pounded together.

She thought how hard and strong his body was in the heat of passion, and now, inside her, holding her, his weight on top of her, she cradled his head and thought how warm and vulnerable he was. She stroked his hair softly.

"If only," she heard herself say.

"Huh?" he looked up at her, raised himself and rested on one hand. "What was that?"

"Nothing," she smiled.

Rob took her hand and kissed it. "Hmmm," he rested it against his cheek," "You smell so good."

It was a little surprising to her that he was so attentive after sex. She had expected him to be up and out. 'There's still time, I suppose,' she thought.

"Is there anything I can get you? Do for you?"

"Well," she raised herself, "you could get my robe. It's over there. I could do with a pee."

Instantly he was on his feet to perform every function for her, tenderly, helping her into her kimono. He treated her as a fragile thing now. Careful and strong and naked in the moonlight, he helped her across the floor to the bathroom door.

"I can take it from her, I really need to tinkle."

He kissed her and grinned, "Tinkle, you're so cute."

"And you're so naked!"

He did a coy act of covering himself up.

In the relative privacy of her bathroom she smiled to herself. The sensations of his stubble against her cheek and the feel of him inside her were still present. She washed herself and checked her face in the mirror. Dead giveaway. Flushed, excited still, and glowing. Jess had never denied herself romantic encounters in her life. She had been with Will for two years. He was a fellow chef. Davie, the ceramic artist, (he of the hair straighteners) was next. He had lasted another two years. This was her pattern. Now and then she had a casual date. Her mother had tried to encourage more of those. But that had never felt right for her. Company and sex at any price were not for her.

For now, Rob was hers, though. He had taken the night off from the life he lived.

Jess opened the bathroom door. The Loft was fully moonlit. Rob stood by the window. He wore his boxer shorts and his work shirt, unbuttoned. She took a moment to enjoy the sight of him. His hand leaned on the frame, he held a mug of tea, and he looked out towards the sea.
"Hi," he looked at her, smiling, "I made a brew," he indicated another cup on the counter. "I hope that's ok?"
She nodded, "For sure." She enjoyed seeing him at ease in her home. He took her hand and helped her to the window seat. He sat behind her, his arms around her and they looked at the night-time seascape together. They sat quietly together, listening. Jess felt supremely happy. She could conceive of a life in the Loft with him. Just the two of them in this oasis, surrounded by the sea at night.
Rob kissed her hair, "You smell good."
She turned to him and their lips met. He kissed her hungrily again. Then he drew back and looked at her, lovingly, in the moonlight. She thought about the stars above them that she had seen when she first climaxed underneath him.

"I can't be with you but I want you. I crave you, Jessie. It's been so difficult being around you. I've thought about you non-stop. I

shouldn't admit this, but that day at the cliffs I had some very – unprofessional thoughts!" He laughed and she hit his arm, playfully. "Skipper! What would your crew say?"
"Don't worry, they gave me hell!"
"So, these inappropriate thoughts? What form did they take?"
"Having to have a beautiful woman harnessed to me? Shall I show you?"
"Yes please!"

She kissed him. Happy, but it was painful to hear him speak these passionate, charming words. She did not want to think about anything beyond tonight, beyond this moment.

Jess decided to take the initiative. She wanted to extract every ounce of pleasure from the night, before it ended. Her one night with him. So, she moved around and sat astride him. Portlyon town and harbour slept outside the windows. He kissed her neck and slid his hands inside her robe. He concentrated on her breasts, slowly and gently. The features she usually felt self-conscious about he seemed more drawn to. Her dark pink nipples and chubby buttocks.
"Your skin is so soft, warm," his lips travelled across her collar bones. She felt his urgent arousal again.

Laughing together, they rid him of his underwear. He eased her onto his lap and she wriggled onto him. Deeper than she had ever felt before. She was breathless with desire. Her silk kimono slipped off her shoulders as they rocked to and fro. He kissed her breasts and she held onto him as the pleasure spasmed through her body.
"Oh god, oh god!"
Rob looked up at her, smiling, "I didn't know you were religious."
"You could convert me."
"Hold on," and he carried her over to the bed.

On top of her he continued to speak her name quietly as she cried out in pleasure. He looked down at her full breasts and held her tightly.
"I can't hold on any longer."

"I want to watch your face," and she drew him deeper into her. He strained and held her with all his strength as his climax hit him.

They relaxed together, kissing and stroking, curled up on the bed. Rob pulled one of the soft blankets to cover them and cradled Jess in his arms. They fell asleep together, warm and blissful.

10 STUNG

Jess sat at the table in the Loft. Her leg was propped up on a stool and she was deep in thought. Paperwork was piled in front of her as she sorted out all her planning for the opening of the restaurant.

There was such a lot to do.

Mathilde was on the other side of the studio at her sewing machine. Lyla was outside, in overalls, painting some signage on the deck. She created distinctive pieces out of driftwood and reclaimed timber, with pastel backgrounds and gold lettering. She had a real flair for design. Matty made good progress with the textiles and soft furnishings. She re-used and upcycled lengths of vintage fabric in a creative way. She possessed the family's artistic ability that had made her brother so famous.

Jess could hear the work going on downstairs as Alastair reinforced joints on the chairs, put up brackets and shelves, and checked all the wiring. She had carefully budgeted for his labour and insisted on paying him, and for all the materials. Matty and Lyla, however, insisted on giving their time for free. Although, Lyla admitted her motive was to gain a good deal per head for the wedding reception. Jess was more than happy to reciprocate. Having a spare pair of hands at this time meant everything to her.

For her supplies, she had been in touch with local producers, brewers, and farmers. Fallon offered to drive her around, whilst her foot slowed her down, to pay visits and check out the quality of what was on offer and make deals. The bakery and patisserie on the High

Street were all geared up for the bread and the desserts. The proprietors, Joanne and Gemma, were excited to be suppliers for a new restaurant venture. There had been local eateries open up nearby but with mixed success. Now that Jess had her property and living space in one, there was a sense of confidence that she could make it work.

What remained for her was the question of logistics. How was she to manage the food service? She was still laid up with her foot, plus she could not take the food outside via the stairs to the dining room. That was too messy, but the kitchen had to be upstairs. She tried puzzling out a solution to this but could not work it out yet. Instead, she turned to the next set of paperwork. Insurance documents. She sighed at the thought of all the red tape. She looked forward to the day when she could employ an assistant. She had to deal with it, though, and found that it was easy enough to get cover as long as she met the conditions. One of these was the need for Health and Safety certification.

Lyla wandered in from her task and began to clean her paintbrushes. Matty stretched and yawned at the sewing machine.
"Tea?" Lyla offered.
"Hmmm – I'm gasping."
Lyla turned to Jess, "Tea?"
"Hmm – huh?" she was preoccupied.
"Anything I can help with?" Matty saw how Jess frowned at the laptop screen.
"I need insurance, and I can receive cover but in order to do that I need a risk assessment by an approved Health and Safety officer. However, that means I have to book one, and of all the local ones the earliest I can find can't make it for another two weeks. That will set everything back, so I'm in a bit of a jam."
She continued to scroll down the website.

"That's not a problem," Matty walked over with a cup of tea. "Rob can sort that out."
Jess had taken a sip of tea and coughed and spluttered at the mention of his name.

"Rob?"

"Yes, he's a Health and Safety person. He has to be because of the boat and the rescue team. He came and did the report for us at the community centre – for free – when we needed to install the new kitchen. He's so sweet!"

"Of course," Lyla agreed enthusiastically. "I'm a part-time TA at the primary school and he's always there helping out. He risk-assessed the PTA summer barbecue."

So, Jess thought, Saint Robert to the rescue again. "What *can't* he do?" she heard herself laughing nervously. She did not want to invite him into her life again. She did not want to rely on him. It had been two days since they had spent the night together. He had said goodbye to her in the morning. He kissed her slowly, longingly, before he left. She really was fully smitten with him, but knew this was the first and only time they could be together. It had to end with that farewell. Now, he was gone. On board the 'Carrie-Ann' and two days out into the Celtic Sea, to follow the herring shoals. It would be at least two more days before he was back in harbour.

All she could hope for was that he returned, and wish him well.

Lyla was talking, "We can ask Christy when she's expecting him home." She reached for her phone to make a call.

Christy – that's her name. The attractive woman from the harbour. Jess felt sick. This was not her, she was not someone who cheated, or who people cheated *with*. But no, she was exactly that now.

"Christy?" Jess asked casually.

"Yes, she lives with him," Lyla was on her phone, the ring tone could be heard in the background and then someone picked up. "Hi, missus!" she laughed. "How's you?"

Rob's 'missus'. Jess felt sick as she listened to the exchange. She heard Lyla confirm with Christy that she would ask Rob as soon as she saw him. She could not contact him when he was out at sea, except by radio.

"Thank you, honey," Lyla was always sweetness itself, "it means sooo much to us all – especially for Jess – to get it all off the ground."

But Jess felt sadness wash over her. She had one stolen night with Rob to last her for the rest of her life. Guilt was blended with a sense of loneliness and absolute misery. Even with things in place, and her new life coming together, there was something absent. The joy of anticipation at creating her own space and livelihood with kind people to help her was tempered by the idea that she had betrayed another woman. In pursuing temporary happiness, she had compromised that of someone else. She had to accept that she was more like her father than she wanted to admit.

After she had filed away the paperwork and restored some order to the Loft, setting Lyla's painted pieces to dry, and Matty had stowed away her sewing machine, Jess hobbled out onto the deck. She felt subdued, anxious, eager to get more work done on the downstairs. The sounds of Alastair working still resonated throughout the Loft. She rested her head in her hands. Matty walked up behind her and rested a hand on her shoulder. Jess started.
"Whatever's the matter, dear girl? Something's not right is it?"
She looked at her aunt, tears filled her eyes and she shook her head.
"No, I'm not all right, Aunty, really I'm not," and she burst into tears. They flowed freely as Matty led her indoors.
"What's wrong? Why are you so sad?"

She sat Jess down and watched her dissolve into sobs.
"Is it your leg? Are you in pain?"
"No, no, it's not that. I'm sad and just so angry with myself. I've been very stupid."
"Whatever's happened?" her aunt was truly distressed and cradled her niece in her arms. Jess's tears eased. Matty dried her eyes with a handkerchief and then looked closely at her. "Tell me why you're so upset."
"I'm so stupid. I shouldn't let it get to me."
Mathilde paused, then she said, "Is it a lad? It's a lad isn't it? Who is it? Someone back in London – someone you miss?"

Jess took the chance for a cover story to explain her sadness. "Yes, I'm upset because of someone I had to leave behind. He broke up with me because I moved." She closed her eyes against the white lie. "Oh darling," her aunt hugged her. "It's painful, I know, leaving someone behind. But if he doesn't want to be here with you, you can't force it. It isn't worth the price of your happiness."

11 MEMENTO

Seagulls stretched their wings above the quay.

Jess looked up at the bright sky on this crisp autumn morning and felt better.

The previous evening, she had poured her heart out to Aunty Matty. She included as much detail as she dared without revealing that the cause of her heartache was close by. She felt relieved that there was no hint of her involvement with Rob circulating amongst the locals of Portlyon. So far. She planned to keep it that way. She had to resist the urge to see him and be alone with him, and that had to begin by ridding her mind of him. Work instead.

She had to pay a visit to the baker's shop to confirm her orders for the opening. The loaves and rolls, warm from the oven and topped with oats or cheese, were delicious and irresistible. The baker, Joanne, was trained to a master level. Her sourdough and the rosemary dinner rolls had an intoxicating scent. Jess held one of the crusty loaves and listened to the sound of the crumb as she pressed it and tapped its base to hear the tempting hollow knock.

Joanne smiled, "It's a lovely batch, isn't it?"
Jess nodded. "I'll take two now. And this is what I'm looking for from opening night onwards. We'll revisit the order regularly. And, I'll also need a tarte tatin, a lemon torte, and a chocolate salted caramel pudding.
"No problem, Gemma will have that all ready." Joanne's sister was the patissière who could conjure up amazing desserts.

"I want to expand, soon, to provide lunch and brunch. Can you supply panini and ciabatta?"

"Of course, plain and flavoured? We have some great specialities."

"Thank you. I'll enjoy collaborating on some new ideas too."

"We're all for that," Joanne helped Jess with her loaves, "let's talk again soon."

Jess hobbled out of the shop.

She had decided to explore the town a little more, in order to follow her physio's instruction to 'mobilise'. If she did not get out of the Loft that day she would have gone crazy. There were too many thoughts and feelings associated with it now. Had that one night of passion spoiled her home for good?

Just that morning, Matty had come over to help out. She had bustled around the room, picking up stray items and then she halted.

"Oh look, a button! And here's another one!" She held in her hand two commonplace shirt buttons. "Where did you come from? I'll save you in my sewing box."

Jess felt a rush of guilty emotion cross her face, and a pang of longing inside. The buttons were from Rob's shirt as he had torn it off in the throes of passion.

When Matty's back was turned she quietly retrieved the buttons from the box.

Instead of dwelling on that moment and the memories of him, she set off down the High Street of Portlyon. She noticed the sign for Simon Evans' second-hand bookshop. The bell above the door rang as she entered. Simon was seated behind the counter on an old wooden swivel chair, specs on his nose, absorbed in a crossword puzzle. Carefully displayed volumes sat on cabinets or were catalogued into subjects on shelves. There was a sense of peace and security here.

He looked up and greeted her.

"Miss Trelawny! How lovely to see you? You don't happen to have another delicious breakfast sandwich with you?" he laughed.

"Not today, but I won't forget for next time. Call me Jess, please."

"And what can I do for you?"

"I wanted to take a look around. I love to browse old cookery books, if you have any?"

"Have a look over there," he indicated a set of shelves in one corner. "You might find some gems."

Jess hobbled across the shop.

"Allow me," and Simon provided her with a stool to sit on. As she scanned the shelves she got talking to him.

"I want to learn more about Portlyon and my father's time here. I know almost nothing about it."

"Well," Simon removed his spectacles, "your father was a local boy. The Trelawnys are an old family around these parts. His father, Colonel Trelawny, married Cecile after the war. She was a great pianist, your grandmother. She had escaped from Paris, as a child, just before the German occupation. I think the rest of her family were lost and scattered. But, Kristof and Mathilde did not get to have an ordinary family life, I'm afraid. Cecile was very unhappy, never recovered from all the loss, I think. She was unsettled and died in a secure hospital when they were just children. Their father sent them away to school."

So, Jess thought to herself as she listened, it sounds as though he was lonely as a boy – lacking his mother, and a father who was distant. I can empathise with that. Simon continued, "He was always so excited when the summer came, knowing that you would be here soon. He used to come in looking for books and comics. He would ask me, 'This year, Jessica is 9,' or, 'this year, Jessica is 10 – what do you recommend for a sophisticated and voracious young reader?' And we would pick out a selection."

"*Those* were from you?"

"Your father chose them with me. I would recommend something and he would say if he thought whether or not Jessica would like it."

"That was one of the best things about my summers here. There was always the box of books and comics by my bed in the Loft when I arrived. It was a treasure trove to explore."

She carried on browsing along the shelves and found an interesting Cornish cookbook.

Simon looked on and smiled.

"You do look like him, you know?"

She grinned back, "So I've been told. He was a handsome devil!"

"He loved you." Simon had a faraway look in his eye. "He was so proud of the drawings he made of you. A catalogue of your years here."

Jess looked at him, bewildered.

"Drawings of *me*?" she shook her head. "I don't think so. Dad never mentioned them and anyway, people were never his subject. He always said he painted landscapes and seascapes because, 'A hill or a boat or a tree will never get upset with you for making them look fat!' The land, sea, and sky, according to him, were honest – people weren't!" She laughed, ruefully. The absences in her life still bothered her but she had learned to deal with them, in a way.

"Well," Simon sounded certain as he rang up her purchase, "he was quite detailed when he spoke of them. Everything he mentioned sounded like it was a labour of love." He handed her the neatly wrapped book. "And after your final summer, when Maxine took over just before he left for France, he worked like a madman. He was shut away in the Loft, no one saw him for weeks. And then, one day, he was gone. Everything removed and locked up. Off to his new life." He looked wistful. "I missed our chats and chess games. We used to enjoy those over a pint of cider. I never got to say goodbye."

Jess squeezed the old man's hand. "I'm sorry. I'm sorry he left like that."

"My dear, don't – nothing whatsoever to do with you. And it must have been hardest of all on you. But, believe me, he did make work inspired by you."

Jess felt better as she left the bookshop, clutching her purchase. Kindness, friendship. Her father had offered that and found it with others, from time to time. Impermanent, but sincere. This gave her a sense of happiness. As for the works Kristof *might* have created, if they even existed, she knew they would be long gone. Maxine, wife-number-three, would have removed them along with everything else

63

as part of her project to claim all of Kristof's works. It was a charming fantasy, rather like her feelings for Rob, that would never come to anything.

She decided she liked Simon. She had a chess-set somewhere. If she brushed up on her skills then she could challenge him to a game.

"Jessie!"
Her heart seized up at the sound of her name. She closed her eyes. Then, she looked around with a forced smile.
"Hello," she managed in reply.
Rob ran over to her. He reached for her, again, for a kiss. She pulled away and saw the now familiar look of bewilderment on his face. He brushed it off, smiling, clearly seeming to think that she did not want to engage in public displays of affection.
"How are you?" he asked quietly.
"Fine," she heard herself being brusque, distant.
"I got your message," he said meaningfully. "I'm meeting Alastair at yours later. I'm so glad you asked me to help out so your place can open."
"Thank you, yes, thank you for agreeing." She felt horribly self-conscious, formal, but really wanted to fall into his arms and feel his touch.
"You know I'd do anything for you. Anything." He smiled and tried to take her hand. She felt too nervous to let him.

"Rob! Robby!" and there was Christy. Attractive, slim, well-groomed Christy trotted over the road and hooked her arm into his.

12 SOLUTIONS

"Christy," Rob greeted her. She wore skinny jeans and expensive boots.

Jess looked down at the chunky walking boot strapped around one leg and the scruffy Converse sneaker on her other foot. She wore her usual shredded denim shorts. She felt the need to get away, quickly.
"Hello," Christy snuggled against Rob. "And who's this?" She looked Jess up and down.
Rob just looked awkward.
"Er ... Christy, this is Jess. Jess, Christy."
"So, *you're* Jess?" she looked her up and down again. "Sending me messages with Lyla, cheeky cow – you're making yourself quite at home, aren't you?" she laughed brightly after this insult.
"Well, this was my home, here and London, for many years. It's good to be back."
"Ooo London! Really?" Christy had a mocking note in her voice and looked from her back to Rob. She clinched his arm in a territorial fashion. Jess noticed that he did nothing to resist.
"It was good to meet you," Jess stepped back. "I have to be going."
"Oh, what a shame." Christy smiled down at her.
"Yes, I have a lot to do."
"I'll see you later," Rob called after her.

She felt weird. She hobbled up the High Street. 'This is not right,' she told herself as she left the couple behind. She resolved to work on the restaurant opening and only deal with him when she had to. He was doing her a favour because of his sister and Lyla, nothing more. Christy would have no reason to suspect anything. She reached the Loft and made her way up the stairs. In a fog of unhappiness. She did not want to think about him anymore.

"Rob's coming around to give me a hand and sort out the safety details – make sure everything is up to scratch." Alastair was in the upstairs studio as she entered. He had made great headway and she was immensely grateful. She still found it difficult to be fully deserving of all the help she received. She was frustrated while she could not manage things on her own, but she felt bad about relying on others. She did not enjoy feeling helpless. Alastair measured up the timber to make the next set of shelves.

Rob arrived. He had followed her, immediately.
"I'm here to help," he smiled at her.
Before she could respond, Alastair slapped him firmly on the back, "That's what I like to hear. He's thinking with his stomach again, aren't you pal?"
Rob staggered forwards at the force Alastair used with his show of approval.
Jess could not help but laugh at this. Rob returned her look with one of pure adoration.
"I'll leave you two alone," Alastair said, "and get on downstairs. See you later."

When he left, Rob came towards her. "Alone at last!" he smiled lovingly. She did not back away so he moved in to kiss her. "You look so beautiful," he said, and took her hand.
"Thank you," she rested a palm on his chest. He was so close. "We need to get on with the safety checks," she looked up at him.
"God, Jessie, I've missed you so much," he breathed.
She could smell him and his mouth was near hers. She saw the blue-back stubble on his chin and around his tender lips. She tried to resist. They needed to talk, arrange things, but he was so close to her. Warm, comforting, tempting.
"We have to get on," Jess closed her eyes and breathed deeply as his mouth found hers. He held her, his hands moved down her body. He kissed her passionately and she felt the desire building. Just a small indulgence, she thought, a short, sweet encounter and then I'll

step away. He kissed her neck and reached down to her hips, pressing against her.

"No," she pulled away from him. "Too much to do."
He rested his forehead against hers, looking into her eyes. "I just want to be around you. Just us."
"Wait," she decided to put an end to this. "It's not working. It isn't right. It's not – we shouldn't be doing this."
He looked confused. She limped away to the window and spoke earnestly and in a low voice. "Both you and I must agree to call this off."
"But, I thought it was going well. That night was amazing." He moved towards her. "Please, talk to me, tell me what's the problem?"
"The problem is – how can you be so – casual about it all?"
"I don't get what you mean? I was respectful to you, wasn't I?"
"I can't believe you don't see anything wrong with this situation."
"So, it's a situation?" he laughed, still confused at her mixed messages.
"Can't you take anything seriously?"
He stepped towards her, "I *am* serious – about *you*."
"No, no way," she backed away, "I'm not letting you get close to me. I won't be caught in the middle of things. I've got too much at stake here to ruin everything over a man."
"What do you mean, caught in the middle? In the middle of what?"

They were trying to keep their voices down but things were getting more heated. Rob's usual friendly, humorous manner was rapidly becoming more passionate, more desperate.

"In the middle of you two – you, and Christy. I'm not getting involved with someone who is cheating! I can't believe you didn't tell me you were with her."
"What?"
"It's undeniable, obvious, now that I've seen you two together. And we moved too quickly. *Way* too quickly. I don't know what I was thinking. And then – then – I find out that you live with someone. You already have someone in your life. And you moved in on me! What kind of person does that?"

"Woah – wait, I never said I was with someone."

"Then who is Christy?" She saw his reaction. "Exactly. You didn't tell me that you lived with her."

"But that's because *she* lives with *me*! I mean – we not together, *together*, the way you think."

"It's made me realise that I know nothing about you. I can't believe how stupid I was to actually sleep with you."

She knew that she was in the wrong, too. She had known he was with Christy but she still decided not to resist the temptation. He looked wounded and she instantly regretted saying all that.

"Guess what, people? I think I've solved it!" Alastair came into the studio. He did not notice the tension in the room. Rob turned away from Jess, bewildered and frustrated. Jess took a deep breath and turned to Alastair with a smile.

"What's that?"

"I've solved the problem of transporting the food – from the kitchen up here to the diners down there."

"How?"

"Come here, Rob mate, give us a hand. Bring a flathead screwdriver and a chisel."

Alastair was in the corner of the Loft, near the end of the kitchen cabinets. He knocked on what looked like a square pillar. It made a hollow thud. He prised a piece of painted hardboard off the side.

"It was clad in this, years ago, and painted over. Here, son," he said to Rob, "give me a hand."

They both got down to stripping the old boards off.

Jess watched what they were doing. She and Rob were temporarily distracted from their shared tension. She became more and more intrigued as they progressed, and excited with what she saw. Behind the cladding was a stone pillar and an inset wooden panel on one side. Alastair and Rob wedged their screwdrivers under the bottom edge of the panel.

"Gently does it, don't force it," Alastair eased the flathead along. "You'll see in a minute," he nodded to Jess. The ancient, thick paint began to flake off and cracked open along the edge of the panel.

"Pass me that block," Alastair pointed to an offcut of timber. Rob wedged it in the gap that had opened up. "Now, along the sides."
The two worked at chipping the paint away and gradually prising the panel up until it could move quiet freely.
"That's incredible – a dumb waiter!" Jess suddenly saw it. "You're right, it's brilliant, *you're* brilliant. The perfect solution. Thank you, thank you."
Alastair laughed at her excitement and said to Rob, "She's easy to please, eh?" as Jess hugged him and kissed his cheek.

Rob looked on with a half-smile on his face, but a sad expression in his eyes.

13 REVELATIONS

A week passed.

The opening night was almost upon them.

Lyla's brightly painted placards were distributed around the town to advertise The Sailmaker's Loft. Jess had planned for a maximum of forty covers for the evening. Compared to her previous jobs in London restaurants it sounded easy, but she knew from experience that would never be the case. On the plus side, it was her menu and her place. She was determined to make it work.

Jess had not spoken to Rob since the day they had found the dumb waiter in the Loft. He had helped Alastair to fully restore it and provided the safety certificate for the insurance company. He had carried out his promises. But she had avoided him. She made sure their paths did not cross, much to Alastair's bewilderment. He sensed something was different but chose not to say anything. When he left for London he hugged her goodbye, with, "It's worth keeping friends, when you're in a new place it's easy to get very lonely, very quickly."

Now, in her chef's whites with twenty-four hours before the soft opening, she was in her element. She tried not to think about Rob. It had been difficult when she went down to the harbour. She had gone to order the fish and could not avoid seeing him. He was aboard the 'Carrie-Ann'. He paused in his work and looked across at her. She halted and their eyes met. He was on deck at a distance and for a few seconds she thought about going to him to try and talk and apologise, perhaps. Instead the fishmonger called over to her to arrange delivery of the fish order for the next day. She turned to him and shook off her feelings of regret to focus on the planning of her menu. She was soon thinking of herb butter and capers to go with the best of the fresh catch. Versatility and simplicity.

No more looks were exchanged before she left.

Back in the Loft she continued with the prep work. The fridge was stocked with the best fresh ingredients and she had made space for the deliveries that were coming in for the next day. A knock at the door. It was Fallon, carrying a box of printed menu cards. Lyla had insisted on creating them.
"Can I offer you a drink?" Jess was glad of the company and the distraction.
"I won't refuse a glass of something interesting."

Fallon was her usual dapper, smart self with her well-tailored clothes that always included a splash of colour. She was in a paisley shirt, trim trousers, and sky-blue brogues. Jess opened a lovely citrusy white wine, an English label. Her aim was to use as many closely sourced products as possible. When she finally got her license and had bar service and a cellar she hoped to use English vineyards and so had a range of delicious samples.

"How's the foot?" Fallon asked cheerfully as she perched on one of the stools at the kitchen counter.
"Getting there," Jess poured the wine and joined her.
Fallon was the sort of person who got straight to the point. She took an approving swig from the glass and opened with, "So, you and my brother. What's the story there, then?"
Jess also took a swig, a large one. "I don't know what you mean?"
Fallon raised a well-sculpted eyebrow and took another mouthful of wine. She moved it around in her mouth and made approving noises. Jess realised that she could not mess this woman around. "Ok, we did have a – date – but it didn't go further than that."

"I knew it!" she clapped her hands. "He has been a nightmare since you arrived! One day he's up and ecstatic, like, really sickening, and then the next day he's an unbearable misery!"

"I don't think that's my doing, it was nothing very serious," but she knew as she said it that it was.

"I tell you what, girl, you're all that's bad for him – and all that's good."

She went on to discuss her brother, and regaled Jess with stories of their childhood.

Jess felt awkward, at first, during this family history, but she continued to listen to the details and the life of the man she had so recently spent the best night of her life with. She began to miss him and want to know him better. Fallon told her how Rob had gone into the family business, out on the boat with his father, at only age sixteen. Their mother died when Fallon was twelve and Rob fourteen. They both had stayed around to support their father.

"Rob held the family together, and went out with the fleet, after Mum. So, I was able to go to college and we all had a living."

"What about him? Did he want to go on with his education?"

"Oh, there was no stopping him once he set his mind on something. He took classes in everything. Brilliant at joinery and engineering, he's also pretty bookish as well. But he can make almost anything and the business relied on him to keep things running. He's mostly practical, but then you'd know all about that!" She smiled slyly. Jess hoped she meant Rob's work on the Loft.

Fallon grew serious, then, "But there haven't been very many women in his life. He doesn't play around."

Jess felt terrible at this, and terrible for Fallon. She did not want to be the one that spoiled her brother's reputation with his friends and family.

"All the things I hear about him tell me he's a decent person. I'm just not ready for any kind of relationship," she lied. In fact, she would have loved more time with him but had to trust the evidence.

Fallon smiled and sipped her wine. "He's been transformed since meeting you. I haven't seen him so happy - not in a long time. Not since Daniel."

"Daniel?"

"Dan was crew on the 'Carrie-Ann'. He worked with Rob and Dad since school. He and Rob were inseparable. So tight."

"And what happened?"

"He drowned, off the North coast, past the rocks out beyond the cove. For someone with so much experience at sea it was just the worst way to go. He took the afternoon out on a pleasure craft with Christy. They'd had a bit to drink and he went over the side. They got into more difficulty and she couldn't get to him."

"That's terrible. He was out with Christy?"

"Yes, his girlfriend. She was devastated of course, a real mess afterwards."

"And Christy is with Rob now?" she said quietly.

"No!" Fallon looked closely at her. "Christy was *Dan's* girlfriend. After he died, Rob stepped in to help her, financially and that's it. Because they hadn't been married the insurance on Dan's life didn't go to her. It went to the business instead."

"But she lives with him now? That's what Lyla said."

"Yes, but he only gave her a place to stay, about a year ago. Rob's got loads of space in our parents' old home. Christy couldn't manage without Dan, she got into money troubles and lost their flat."

"That's terrible, I had no idea."

"Well, you weren't to know, and you've got to feel for her. But, she *is* a bit difficult. It's hard to feel sorry for her sometimes. She's been brave, but *very* demanding. Rob stepped in to save the day, but now she leans on him. He's put her up but there's no sign of her leaving. Now, he feels that if he asked her to move out it would be cruel."

Jess listened and processed all this.

"So, Christy and Rob aren't a couple?"

"Not at all!" Fallon laughed. "She isn't his type, as well you know!"

Jess ignored the potentially embarrassing topic and however painful it felt, she pursued it. "But, she does act as though they are a couple. She's very – possessive - over him."

Fallon topped up her glass, "Christy would *like* for something to happen between them. And, for sure, I think she's tried it on. But Rob would never say anything, he's too kind. Sometimes a bit of a pushover."

"She seems to be very sure of herself, and him."

"Look," Fallon was passionate, blunt, "never mind about her. I know my brother and I've seen the effect you've had on him. I haven't seen him so happy. Just re-consider, maybe? If there's no hope – tell him – but if you can, throw him a bone, eh!?" she laughed.

Jess closed her eyes and smiled at the memory of Rob at the Loft.

"I don't know," she paused, then said, "I do like him – God, yes, I like him. But the idea that he was with someone else made me back away. I never meant to hurt him."

Fallon, a little tipsy now with the good wine, jumped off her stool and hugged Jess.

"I can see you're a good person, I want us to be friends."

"Me too!"

"And if the fact that my – idiot – brother is in reality single, despite appearances to the contrary, and that means you *might* think about him in a different way, that's wonderful!"

After Fallon had made her, prolonged, farewells Jess was left with a good feeling. Better than she had in a long time. She realised that a feeling of ease in her life, with good friends, and no game-playing helped make everything better. No matter the successful business or the amount of money, loneliness and lies made everything worse. She had seen enough of that over the years, with her mother and her life in London. Huge acclaim and wealth had come along for people she knew in her industry but that did not mean anything without love, company, or someone to care for. Obvious, but nonetheless sometimes hard to achieve.

In Portlyon, Jess had started to discover a community, from Joanne the baker to Simon in the bookshop, to actual family with Matty. Lyla and Fallon, she could think of as family – but she dared not. That would mean Rob, and things working out with him. Beyond her grasp, she was sure. Jess decided not to think about that. She thought about the opening tomorrow. I will work through that, she thought, and then we'll see.

14 SWEET-BITTER

Jess Trelawny was hitting her stride. The layout of her Loft kitchen was working out for her. Lyla was proving herself as a competent kitchen assistant, or 'wench' as she insisted on being called: "I am your official lackey, your kitchen wench," she declared.

Downstairs, Matty took orders and relayed them via iPad up to the kitchen. Jess and Lyla worked on getting them out in the dumb waiter to the cosy dining room. Dirty dishes came back up and into the washer.

"This is fun!" Lyla rotated the handle of the dumb waiter. "Who knew a pulley and a tray could be so entertaining?"

"I hope the novelty doesn't wear off!" Jess joked from where she was busy at the range.

"It's working so well, we're getting a great production going here and I'm having a work-out."

The menu was fresh and exciting, fun and interesting and full of local produce. Jess felt happy as she prepared and sent the food out. The opening of the Sailmaker's Loft had started on an anxious note a couple of hours earlier. With the prep completed, Jess had waited with Lyla on the deck overlooking the harbour and the yard. Matty put the finishing touches to the tables downstairs. With Matty on hand, as maître d extraordinary, she had complete faith in the welcome the customers would receive and the aesthetic of their dining experience.

But, seven o'clock rolled around and no one showed up.

Jess chewed her lip and felt doubts creeping over her. 'No one here wants this. I'm Kristof's daughter and they aren't impressed with me. As well as which, if rumours circulate about me and Rob, everyone's sympathy with be for Christy. The fisherman's widow.' Jess's thoughts had run on.
Lyla noticed her concern. "Don't worry. They *will* come."

Fallon arrived, with her camera. She was compiling material for the Loft's website. She had worked out a great deal with Jess, to build the site and keep it up-to-date. Jess was happy that it would involve lots of beautiful images of Lyla.

Gradually, however, customers started to filter in. First, Simon with his wife, Rosanna. Joanne, Gemma, and their partners came next. Fallon's employees, and by seven thirty, there were three or four tables filled and Jess had things well under way in the kitchen. By eight thirty, Matty messaged up to them, "We've hit capacity. I've got people waiting for tables. Can we do a limited second sitting? And is it ok to take bookings for tomorrow night?"
Jess wiped her brow and signalled to Lyla to message her, 'Yes'. She limped from one surface to another, her mobility was fortunately improved with the light-weight boot supporting her injury now.

The evening continued in a hectic blur, like all the best services, full of fragrance and flavour. Things flowed smoothly and it was not until almost the very end of the evening that she remembered how much her ankle hurt. She rested on a chair by the window and enjoyed a cup of tea whilst Lyla sent out the last of the desserts. Then she joined her.
"Did you enjoy that?"
"Loved it," she sighed. "I feel like I'm getting back to normal. How about you?"
Lyla smiled. Fallon came up to join them. She kissed her exhausted but happy fiancée.
"It was great," Lyla declared. "I loved watching you work. I loved every minute of it in fact."

"Looks like you've got yourself a permanent kitchen skivvy."
Lyla thwacked Fallon with a tea-towel, "Skivvy? I'll have you know
I'm a kitchen wench."
They all laughed, relaxed and happy. Good company, Jess thought,
and a sense that this could become her home. She cautiously felt she
could belong here.

It was at this point, inevitably, that her thoughts turned to Rob. She
wondered where he was, what he was up to, what he was thinking
tonight. Maybe she would see him? Maybe she could go and talk to
him? Now that she knew the extent of his real relationship with
Christy, maybe she could start afresh with him?

Fallon was talking, "So, are you ready to greet your public? There
were so many compliments to the chef that Matty was overwhelmed.
She made me promise to get you down there."
"Go on, go on!" Lyla urged.
"You have to come too! We're a team."
"Oh, I love that!"

Jess and Lyla entered the dining room to a round of applause. Matty
hugged both of them. Fallon snapped some pictures.
It was Jess's turn to feel overwhelmed and flattered.
"I *love* this!" Lyla was in her element and squeezed Jess's hand. "Is it
always like this?"
Jess laughed and shook her head, "Er, no! Think again."
As everyone celebrated with them, Jess looked hopefully around the
room. No sign of him. That is, until two people moved around a
table and he came into view. She was surprised by his presence and
he noticed her colour change. Both of them knew he was sitting at
the very spot, near the fireplace, where their first passionate
encounter had taken place. She tried to smile in his direction but
more people milled in between them, congratulating her, and she
lost sight of him.

When the way was cleared again, Jess saw, with an emotional lurch,
that Christy was sitting opposite him at the corner table. He leaned
towards her, and they spoke confidentially. Christy laughed. Jess felt

a pang of intense sorrow, and yes, jealousy. He had been there all along, with her, in the restaurant. He was just downstairs from where Jess had been putting her heart and soul into her new business.

He looked around at her and their eyes met. There was an expression from him that she could not quite interpret. Then he smiled and mouthed to her, "Well done."
She felt like crying. She nodded in acknowledgement and gave him a brave smile. Then she was swept away on a wave of warmth and friendship, answering questions and accepting a celebratory glass of bubbly. When she looked back at the table, Rob and Christy were gone.

Despite the party atmosphere, she remained calm and quiet. As soon as she could free herself she went back upstairs for the clean down. She worked her way across all the surfaces, shelves, equipment, and ovens. It was therapeutic and automatic for her. She found it comforting, it put her in control. Inside the kitchen she was the boss. Outside, well that was a different matter, and she was still uncertain and full of trepidation about the turbulence of the emotions and feelings involved.

Lyla and Fallon helped in the dining room and Matty swept up.

Soon, chairs were perched on the tables, the dishwasher rumbled silently, and the moonlight glinted off the stainless steel in the Sailmaker's Loft.

15 CHOICES

Jess decided, with Lyla's input, that the Loft would officially open for dinner only, starting on a Thursday, Friday, and Saturday evenings. She took bookings throughout the week and hired some ad space in local media. Two weeks passed and they settled into a regular pattern of working, deliveries, prep, service, and clean down.

She was glad to be out of the way and busy in the upper floor of the Loft, so that just in case Rob showed up again with *her*, she did not have to witness anything that passed between them. Dinners for two, and *not* in a relationship? It felt too awkward for her.

Lyla handled bookings through the website and helped to keep the menus up to date. She had even started a Sailmaker's Loft Twitter account and Facebook page. Jess was glad she enjoyed doing it and was happy for her to get on with it. During the day, her major task was to research and develop new ingredients and recipes as well as handle the paperwork. She continuously thought about how she could make improvements to the restaurant and how to transition the menu across the seasons. She had begun to feel part of Portlyon. That feeling from the summer holidays in her childhood started to revisit her. Every now and then, a memory or sensation flickered into her mind and a sense of peace and comfort came over her. She did feel lonely though, part loneliness, part nostalgic. There had been a slight chance at happiness with someone, as it was with her father, but that was snatched away. She had grown used to that in her life. Chances missed.

The lovely, passionate episodes she had enjoyed were still with her, but fading away. She had misread and misjudged him. She had thought such a passionate, attentive, funny man interested in *her* was too good to be true. Abandonment issues, I suppose, she thought. I'll have to address those one day. But, not now. Now, I have my business.

Jess's lightweight boot made it easier to move around. It gave her enough support without the clumsiness. Two more weeks, the physio told her. Every day it got easier but seemed never-ending. She was so bored now and ready to move on.

Every morning she walked a little further. She went as far as Joanne's bakery. She had a good routine with the baker and her sister, Gemma, the patissière. New flavours could be introduced and tested out at tastings. It turned out that Joanne was quite experimental in her approach and she enjoyed trying out new ideas. They had a turmeric and cardamom dinner roll, sprinkled with garlic salt, and the customers loved them. Now, Jess wanted to try something with saffron. She thought about offering saffron bread, a traditional Cornish delicacy.

Joanne made some suggestions, "We could try something at the savoury end, as well as go with the traditional recipe with raisins, sultanas, and spices."
The shop bell rang behind Jess. She did not look round. She was absorbed in the feel and smell of the fresh bread in front of her. Joanne looked up, "I'll be with you in a minute."
Jess felt the pleasant, yielding crumb of one of the rolls, and took in the fresh-baked smell, "Hmm," she made a pleasured noise, "that's amazing."
A familiar voice behind her made her freeze, and blush to her roots at being caught making little moaning sounds over fresh bread.
"May I try one?" Rob was right beside her.

She quickly put the bread roll down. She heard herself say, "I'm interested in both, we could try them, if you don't mind?"

"I'd love to, I've wanted to experiment with some saffron recipes for some time, but it's expensive stuff!" Then Joanne turned to Rob, "Of course, help yourself to a sample."

"Thank you," Jess gathered up her purchases and sought to bundle them out of the small shop, skirting around him. She had parcels containing crusty rolls and some sourdough loaves. She had to turn, and she took a deep breath as she looked up at him.

"Hello," he said.

"Hello," she breathed.

"Can I help you with that?" he offered.

"No, thank you. I'm fine."

Joanne looked at them both and quickly busied herself with another task. Rob stepped aside. The shop was small, so she had to squeeze past him with her parcels.

"Sorry," he stepped to one side.

"Sorry," she stepped to the other side. He let her pass.

Jess edged her way out of the shop and stood on the pavement outside. She started to limp up the road and when she was several yards along a bag of saffron buns escaped from her purchases. They plopped onto the pavement, still in the bag, and threatened to roll away.

"Oh no," she cursed. Her hands were full and she could not stoop down.

"It's ok, I've got them," Rob was right behind her. He gathered them up and perched them back on top of her packages. "Nice looking buns," he grinned.

She flared a look at him.

"I'm being insolent, sorry. It's very fine to see you, Jessica." He went all formal and she felt self-conscious.

"You too," she nodded.

"Please, let me help you home."

"No, it's ok really."

"I insist," and he stepped closer to her and took the bag from her. "Here," he said, "you grab the buns."

She looked sideways at him and he returned her glance with a mischievous wink.
"You just can't help yourself, can you?"
"Was that a smile I detected?"
She broke into a grin and looked away.
"Ah, there it is!"

They turned the corner together into Sailmaker's Yard.
"This is me."
Rob paused and looked down at her, smiling, "I'll be going, shall I?"
She hesitated, then said, "Do you want to come up? I'll put the kettle on."
"Does that mean what I hope it means?"
"That depends, what are you hoping for?"
"One of these delicious buns with a cuppa."
They walked up the stairs to the Loft, laughing.

Below them, unseen in the Yard, Christy observed the goings-on and their relaxed exchange.

16 BROKEN

Jess felt excited but also very contented at the idea that Rob was with her in the Loft again.

She unpacked her purchases from Joanne's bakery. Rob wolfed down one of the saffron buns as soon as she handed it to him. He looked cute.

"I haven't eaten anything all day."

"It's only ten-thirty," she laughed.

"Well, not since breakfast."

Jess bit into a luscious carrot cake muffin.

Rob smiled, "Here, allow me," and he wiped the dab of frosting from the tip of her nose. She put the cupcake down and moved around the counter top towards him. He took her in his arms, joyfully.

They held one another for a few moments. Here was the peace she craved.

"Hello, you," he breathed in happily.

"I'm so sorry about the things I said."

"You have nothing to be sorry about."

"I shouldn't have said those things."

"I should have told you about Christy and been up front, so that you could understand. If that's possible," he added, "because even I don't understand the situation."

"I get it now, and I have Fallon to thank. She explained it all to me."

"I have so much to thank Fallon for! It gave me hope. When she told me that you hadn't ruled out ever seeing me again."

"I'm thankful for her intervention. I had no idea that you'd done so much for your friend. And I understand why you wouldn't tell me. But I want you to – tell me everything about yourself and your life, and friendships. She said that you and Dan were very close. I'm sorry."

"He was like a brother to me, we were very close. But I want to talk about you and me." He nuzzled into her neck.

"I wish I had known you were here on opening night."

"Why? What would you have done? Poisoned my starter?"

She punched him, playfully, "You're terrible."

"But you love it!"

Rob and Jess paused and looked into each other's eyes. He started to kiss her, "God, I have really missed you." He lifted her up in his arms. They moved quickly to the bed and fell on it together, laughing.

"Ow, ow!" his forehead bumped her chin.

"Sorry, sorry!" and he smothered her face and neck with kisses.

"It's ok," she snuggled into him.

They lay quietly together for a few minutes, exchanging occasional kisses and relishing the quietness together. Jess rested her head against his chest, with its soft, warm lamb's wool jumper. The perfect temperature when there was a slight chill in the air. She snuggled deeper into him and sighed.

"Don't hold back," he kissed the top of her head, "get closer." He smelled the fragrance of her hair, "Hmmmm, strawberries."

She laughed and sat up to smell his hair, "Hmmm, herring!"

"Well, it's fortunate I'm dating a chef who will never mind the smell of a fisherman."

"And, are we? Dating?"

He rested on one arm and took her hand in his. "Do you want to? Do you want me to be your boyfriend?"

She smiled as he reached for her. One hand went to the back of her head and he began to kiss her gently, then passionately and more hungrily. He pulled her on top of him and she lay along his body.

"This is where I need to be," he stroked her hair and his other hand moved down her body. His hand rested on her buttock and she squirmed a little in delight and pressed against him. He kneaded one cheek and moved his hand down to the other. Taking both of her buttocks he massaged them, urgently, and she felt a tingling all up and down her body and began to melt into him.

Jess could feel Rob's need for her again. She raised herself and climbed off him, more mobile than she had been the first time they were together. She reached for his belt and flies. He pulled his jumper off, eager to be unclothed with her, as she unfastened his trousers.
"I want you so much," his voice was husky with desire.
She smiled and removed his trousers. He reached for her but she held him off, gently. "No, she said, "let me." He looked a little bewildered at this until he saw her move down his body, kissing, stroking him lightly, and then she took him in her mouth.
"Oh, oh my gosh!" he gasped out.
She smiled and kissed him gently. Then, with mouth and fingers she brought him to an even greater level of arousal. She paused to ask him, "Is this ok? Tell me if I hurt you."
"It's just," he stammered, "I've never …".
"Never? Really?"
He shook his head, "Nice Cornish lasses don't do this sort of thing!"
"Not like us bad London girls, obviously!"
"Oh, yes," he breathed, "I like bad girls!"

Jess giggled and recommenced her gentle actions. Gradually, steadily, she grew more vigorous and looked up at him. The sight of her large, blue eyes, tousled hair, and sensual red lips around him made him moan and shudder with pleasure. He threw his head back and grasped the coverlet with one hand, he held her gently with the other. She worked him faster, bore down on him, until, trembling, he climaxed with a shout.

Afterwards, she lay in his arms. He held her tight, kissing her, kissing her.
"Are you ok?" she smoothed his hair.
"I thought my heart would burst," and he kissed her again.

Suddenly, the alert from his pager broke into their peace.

"What? You're joking!" she leaped up.

"Quick, my trousers. I don't think I can stand yet."

She hurriedly retrieved his clothes and, trying to be serious, helped him to dress. "This is getting a little like a French farce," she could not help herself.

He paused and kissed her. Their hungry, good-bye kiss. "I'll be back soon. Wait here!"

"Take care! Take care!"

"Always," he grinned and was out of the door.

Jess watched him race to the launch. Her heart started to ache.

'I will have to get used to this, I suppose,' she thought. Then smiled at the idea of his bravery. He was so kind and capable, she mused. How could he not be with someone amazing already – someone like him? Perhaps it was the demands of being out with the fishing fleet and off with the crew of the lifeboat? Unpredictable, self-sacrificing. Some people just do not want that. But she felt that it was too good to be true, in her life.

She saw his sweater, left on her bed. She rejoiced a little at the sight of it. So normal and ordinary, as though it belonged there. Yes, she thought, my boyfriend. She went to the door with it but he was long gone. So, she held on to it and breathed in his smell.

Jess buried her face in the soft wool and he was with her again. Blushing to herself she recalled what she had just done and his reaction to it. She pulled the garment on, so that she could be surrounded by him whilst he was gone. She turned back to the kitchen counter.

"Christy!" she looked amazed at the woman standing there. "Where did you come from?"

"I tried knocking," she spoke sweetly, "but there was no answer. I think you were busy."

Jess had a chill run all over her. Had Christy been watching them when - ? The question went through her mind and she dreaded the answer.

Christy took her time and walked around the Loft, sauntering in a critical fashion. She looked along the shelves and the kitchen counter.

"Nice set-up you have here," and she picked up a salt mill. She turned the smooth, white ceramic over in her hands.

"I didn't hear you knock," Jess eyed her suspiciously. "Tell me what you want, or leave. I'm very busy."

Christy paused. "Busy, busy, busy – yes – busy, little Jessica."

"What?"

Christy placed the ceramic mill on the counter, and to Jess's astonishment, she deliberately, slowly, slid it off the side to make it smash on the floor at her feet. Shards of broken pottery and sea salt crystals went everywhere.

"Oops!" and she smirked at Jess.

Jessica was not having any of this.

"Get out of here. Just leave. This is my home, and I don't want you here."

"This will never be your home," Christy shook her head, laughing. "Don't you get it?" and she walked towards Jess, who felt her anger rising. "You're not welcome here, no one wants you – especially not Rob!" She stood before Jess, hands on hips. "*I'm* what he needs and *we* are going to be together," she spoke slowly as if Jess were a foolish child. "That night – the opening of your fancy restaurant – he slept with me. Yes, that's right. We had sex. And your food was pretty rubbish too, by the way."

Jess shook her head.

"Oh, yes he did. He told me he thought his heart was going to burst!"

Jess looked away and closed her eyes, then she said, "I've had enough of this."

"Too difficult to hear? Rob likes to deceive women, but I know him and I can let him have his fun. Because, I know it's *me* he really wants. He's only trying to show some respect for Danny, but we'll be together. He comes home to *me*. So, you need to leave."

Jess paused, and then with her mouth set, she strode towards Christy. The other woman was not expecting this.

"NO," she said, "*you* need to leave," and she gripped a clump of long, sleek hair at her scalp.

"Ow, ow, you're hurting me!" the woman protested.

"No, I'm not. Not yet. But I will if you struggle or try to resist." She reached the Loft door with the squirming Christy and opened it. "You think you can come into *my* place and insult *my* food?" She thrust her out of the door and onto the deck at the top of the stairs. "Now, get out of my house and don't even think of coming back."

"How dare you? You bitch!"

"Oh, I dare, I definitely dare!" She stood at the top of the stairs as Christy started to stumble her way down. "You're barred!"

Back inside, hot with anger, Jess tried to calm herself as she cleared up the mess. What an absolute lunatic, she thought. She is deranged. But, she had better not be telling the truth. "It's not my business, of course," she said aloud, "what he got up to." She was nevertheless disturbed by Christy's actions and her desire to lay claim to Rob. She felt angry, confused, and upset. Not with Rob, he was out at sea, risking his life. She did not want to fall for him and have to face more upset. Risks, risks came with him.

So, she decided to distract herself with some work. She fixed up the orders for the next day. "I can't torment myself with any of it," she said to herself, "until he's back and I can speak to him." No more lies, no more nonsense, or avoiding the truth, she decided. If he wants to have me in his life, if he is my 'boyfriend' now, then he has to get rid of the crazy lady!

She was contemplating this further when her phone rang. The display told her it was a London number. She answered.

"Hello!" a voice on the other end before she could say anything. "Is this Jess – Jess Trelawny, I'm speaking to? This is Duncan Spalding from the Mercury website. I'm the editor of the 'What's Hot?' feature and I'd like to talk to you about your new restaurant."

"Go on," Jess was interested.

17 RESTORED

No word.

Usually the update came into the Coastguard station.

No word.

Fallon rang Jess. Had she heard anything? Was there a message from Rob? The Portlyon lifeboat was still logged as 'out'. It was unusual, she told Jess, for there to be radio silence for this long. It had to mean something serious.

Jess joined Fallon on the quayside in the late afternoon. Matty cycled up a few minutes later, her headscarf flapping in the swirling breeze. The three women waited there and looked out to sea as the light faded. The weather had been calm inland and at the harbour when the call came out for the rescue. Now, dark clouds billowed across Portlyon from the horizon, and blustery winds grew.

Paul from the 'Carrie-Ann' came over.
"Any word?" asked Fallon.
He shook his head, grimly.
Jess felt sick to her stomach at the monosyllabic restraint. She looked out at the harbour and the roiling sea beyond the wall. The heavy, slate sky threatened them and the atmosphere felt grim, as twilight advanced. Out at sea, the weather grew worse.

Still, no word.

The Air Sea Rescue chopper broke through the rushing wind and the sea spray in the air above. It banked to fly along the coastline to the west into the watery glow of the setting sun beneath the clouds. Jess felt afraid. She knew for sure now – nothing else mattered – only Rob's safe return. Nothing else meant anything – not Christy – none of it. So what, if they had slept together? He wasn't with me then, she reminded herself, not my boyfriend, as he is now. He wants to be with me now. She just wanted him back, safe with her at the Loft. At home.

Fallon noticed her quiet concern. She put an arm around Jess's shoulder.
"How are you feeling?"
"How do you get used to this? You must worry for your brother all the time."
"You never really get used to it. But there is a way of handling it. And you need to realise that he is bloody good at what he does. He *will* come home."
They hugged.
"I hope – I know – he will."

Fallon and Matty walked back to the Loft with her and bid goodnight. On her own, as the late autumn storm worsened, Jess put a lamp in the window. Night fell and the stars tried to glint between dark clouds that raced above the inky sea.

Eventually, Jess curled up in her clothes beneath a fleece blanket on the divan. She kept the blinds of the Loft open and the single lamp lit. Waiting. Waiting, until she slept.

It must have been in the early hours when Jess woke to a slight sound. She rose quickly and was able to place the noise through the blur of sleep. A tapping at the door. She wrapped her blanket around her and, barefoot, made her way across the Loft's wooden floor in the light of the lamp. An imposing figure stood outside in the darkness. She opened the door and, with a thrill of relief, saw Rob

91

standing there. He was still in his full weather-proof gear, like an exhausted, embattled warrior emerging from the shadows to come home.

"Your light was on," his dark eyes looked exhausted, right into her soul, and his voice was quiet and husky.

"Always," she murmured and kissed his lips, still with their taste of seawater, trembling and grateful.

Rob half fell into her arms. She led him inside to the bed.

Some hours later, towards dawn, Jess awoke. For a few moments she felt confused, and then remembered. The weight across her body was Rob's arm and he was curled around her. His face was close to the back of her neck and she lay still, feeling the sensation of his body and breath against her. Now, she felt perfect bliss. She remembered waking up, in this very room, after a long journey from London as a girl. After the adjustment, came the knowledge that there was no school and weeks of carefree summer holiday lay ahead. This had been the greatest feeling on first opening her eyes. Until now.

Carefully, so as not to disturb him, she turned over so she could see Rob's face in the early light. His dark brows, strong features, messy bed-hair, and full growth on his chin. She took everything in. She studied him, so as to remember all the details. He stirred slightly, and murmured her name. Her heart nearly burst with joy to realise she was in his dreams.

Exhausted and silent when he arrived at her door, she had helped him onto the bed and out of his gear. By the time his boots were off he was barely sitting up. Wordlessly, she held his face in her hands and saw the strain and fear that possessed his eyes after what he had been through. They kissed quietly, and then curled up together like hibernating animals under the woollen coverlet.

The chilly morning. Jess wriggled out from under the covers. Rob rolled over with a sigh. She looked at him, love filled her heart. Quietly, she used the bathroom, freshened up, and put a pot of coffee on. She was only in cotton shorts and a t-shirt so she started to shiver. She quickly snuggled under the covers again.

Rob was awake now and looking at her.
"Good morning," he spoke quietly, seriously.
He too had a serious look in his eyes. "Come here," and he reached for her, pulled her towards him. He kissed her over and over, hungrily, his hands roaming over her body. She felt his urgency. His passion was desperate, rapid.
"You must be tired, still," she gasped, "there's no need to hurry."
He looked deep into her eyes, his passion dark and determined. "Yes, yes there is," he insisted, breathing hard, "I need to be inside you."
She melted into him. He kissed her harder and harder, painfully, and then they were grappling at their clothing, pulling off underwear until they were pressed together, warm and naked. Jess felt electric shocks running through her body. His desire mounted and he rolled on top of her, looking down at her breasts, he sucked on one and then the other. She moaned aloud, "Oh, oh!"
Rob smiled down at her pleasure, and thrust hard inside her. She was warm, wet and ready, but still it made her gasp and cry out in slight pain. He was rock hard and stabbed into her softness.

He stroked and kissed her as their hips rocked together, rhythmically and steadily, a mixture of urgency and gentleness. He clasped one of her hands against his chest, their faces close together, and her climax built.
"I want to look into your eyes when you come," he whispered. She cried out as she orgasmed. He kissed her passionately again and again. "Jessie, Jessie," his mouth moved down to her breasts, sucking and nibbling on them. Her nipples puckered dark pink as he caressed them further, licking and tugging.

Rob began to push into her again, gazing into her eyes. She wrapped her legs around him to pull him deeper inside her and he gripped her buttocks. He pumped harder and harder. She gasped, it was so strong it began to hurt a little. Some pain mingled with pleasure. Exquisite. She came loudly again, her orgasm overwhelming her. She expected him to stop or at least ease up but he grew even more earnest. He knelt on the bed and lifted her legs and hips up. The change in position caused her to spasm and climax again.

"I want you to come again and again," he grunted as he pounded into her, all the anguish, desire, and frustration of the last twenty-four hours mounting inside him. "Jessie, I love you, I love you!"

Jess shouted again as the pleasure swept over her. He collapsed onto her. "You're so beautiful when that happens."
"It's still happening," she could feel it washing over her.
He thrust to finish and grimaced as he did so. "Jessie, oh God, I love you so much." He kissed her, staying inside her, panting and stroking her. She wriggled against him, nibbled his ear, and felt him inside her, still filling her. He rubbed her breasts.
"Are you ok?"
She thought about what he had cried out in his passion, "Uh huh," she nodded.
"I missed you."
"I got that impression. I was so worried about you. When there was no word."
"Shh," he put his finger gently to her lips, "we don't talk shop when we make love."
She laughed, "Ok! Is that the rule from now on?"
He hugged her and breathed her scent.
"But I wanted you to know how much I cared and how fearful I was."
"I was too!" he smiled.
"Everyone said you'd be ok, that you know what you're doing."
"And do you agree? Do I know what I'm doing?"
"Hmm," she nuzzled into his neck, "pretty good."

Rob had not pulled out of her, and now she felt him starting to get hard again. He moved gently and slowly at first. She looked at him, "Impressive," she sighed.
"Thank you," he kissed her.

Later on, they enjoyed some coffee and then Rob insisted on making breakfast.

"You cook all the time, for everyone. I want to spoil you."
She lay on her stomach on the bed and watched him. The radio
played as he scrambled eggs and grilled bacon. She knew then that
she loved him too.

A life stretched before her, in Portlyon with Rob. Maybe? For the
first time, she dared to plant an idea about her future.

When everything was ready, he held the chair out for her and flicked
the seat with a tea-towel before she sat down.
"First," he kissed her with a stubbly chin that rubbed her face.
"Hmmm, delicious," she sighed.
"Now," he poured orange juice, "I opened the carton myself."
"Delicious," she smiled, "so piquant!"
Then he served up toast, bacon, eggs, and coffee. The toast was
singed, the bacon was a little too crispy, the eggs were messy but it
was the most delicious meal that Jess had ever tasted.
They both ate, heartily and ravenously. When they finished, he
cleared away and they made love again in the clear morning. Rob fell
asleep in her arms, peaceful and calm.

He had told her over breakfast just how tough the night's rescue had
been. A fishing boat had lost power and was drifting in the storm,
with some injured crew on board. That's all he would say, the barest
of details. It took the lifeboat a long time to return because they were
sent further up the coast to transport the crew to the closest harbour,
whilst the helicopter took the injured to the hospital in Truro.

As Jess watched him sleep she tried to process the feelings that she
had previously pushed aside but now came to the fore.

18 LOVE

Jess worked on preparation for the restaurant service during the afternoon. She could not help but feel a glow as she peeled the vegetables and began to cook the pork belly for the evening's special. Rob had left for the harbour, reluctantly, but she insisted he leave and check in with his sister who had only had a text message to allay her fears so far. Fallon had replied that she was relieved to hear he was safe, but she understood he was too busy to visit her.

Rob kept kissing her, and acted agonised about having to leave as Jess removed him from the Loft. They both laughed as she prised his fingers off the wooden rail of the stairs. She felt supremely happy, at last.
"Go away – go away!" she whacked him with her kitchen cloth. "I have to work, and so do you."
"Can I come back for my dinner?"
"Of course, you get to eat for free – as long as,"
"What? I provide favours for the chef?"
"Hmm, something like that. You must please me."
They kissed goodbye, again.
"I think that can be arranged, but I feel so used! I must perform for my supper."
"Yes," and she spanked him playfully on the bottom as he turned to leave.
"I'm gonna get so fat," she heard him say, to her delight.

Well into prep for that evening's service and Jess's phone rang. She wiped her hands and swiped the screen.

It was Duncan Spalding.

"I'm not disturbing you, am I?" But he did not wait for her answer and just launched into, "My assistant ate with you last week and she has not stopped raving about the menu, the setting, everything, since then. Please say I can interview you and your team this weekend?"
"I have dinner service tonight, so tomorrow – Sunday?"
"Fantastic. I'll be down tonight with my people, so we want a table. We'll dine, we'll enjoy your amazing food and then we take over tomorrow. You're mine! I'll have hair and make-up coming – the whole works. You're my everything and I couldn't be more excited."

After this breathless, one-sided conversation, Jess felt tired. She mused on this revisiting of the hoopla and fuss of a London media crowd. She was Duncan's new, exciting find this week. She knew that meant being a hot media item would last for a few weeks and she would be swiftly forgotten by the London visitors. This suited her now. The reason she wanted her own place was not for attention or fame, or passing fashion. Good publicity was very welcome, however. She was aware that it would move on. Her reason for returning to Portlyon was to create something permanent.

That evening, service ran smoothly for Lyla and Jess. Saturdays were busy, and with Duncan and his team arriving from London, they had a full house. Matty was the usual delightful maître d, amusing all the VIPs.

After the last customer left and the clean-down was under way, Jess chatted to Lyla.
"So, you're ok for coming in tomorrow morning? You don't mind being part of the feature?"
"Are you kidding? This sounds mad. But, I'm a fraud, I'm not in the 'trade'."
"Silly – you're great. I've worked with so many people and I can tell a natural when I meet one. With cooking, you can learn on the job."
"You really think so?"

"Yes, you have the touch and the passion. I want you to be there. Have you thought about creating some main courses? What would you like to offer the customers?"

"Me – cook mains? Really?" Lyla excitedly collected her things, "I'll have to start my research! I have some ideas."

"See you tomorrow, then. Around ten?"

"Try and stop me."

Jess finished the clearing and decided to turn in before the big day.

After he had eaten, Rob promised he would be back. He had to see to the equipment at the station. She was excited to see him, as always, with a knot of anticipation in the pit of her stomach. But, she was also bothered with the idea of the unspoken subjects between them. The first and most unpleasant was Christy. The second, happier one, was that he had told Jess he loved her.

She sat down and removed her ankle support. The ligaments were nearly heeled and she looked back on the past couple of months with some happiness and bewilderment. She remembered the sickening fall on the cliff face. And then Rob, and how she felt nervous and embarrassed about being rescued, but he had only cared about her.

Rob arrived. He got down on one knee – to massage her foot. He kissed her instep.

"You have lovely feet."

"Please don't spend too long considering them – even though that feels really good – I've been standing on it throughout service and it must be whiffy."

He scooped her up in his arms and carried her to the bed.

"I'm really going to have to change these sheets," she looked down. Rob kissed her and let his hands roam down her body. "Let's make the most of these in the meantime then," and he leaped onto the bed beside her, charming her instantly with his boyish grin. "And then," he laughed, "we should preserve them, as a memento of our love-making."

"Ooh no!" Jess cowered at the idea. "I'd prefer a flower pressed in a book, anything?"

She paused as he kissed her. Comforting and passionate. She felt the need for him again. But she knew she needed to talk about what was on her mind.

"This question of our 'love'?"

"Yes?"

"Was this something uttered in the moment? Or?"

He took her hand and kissed the tips of her fingers.

"What would you say if it was – more? More than just a passion of the moment?"

She was silent. He looked at her, curious, and then, "Well?"

"You, are in love - with me?"

"Yes," he said, boldly, "I am. I love you, Jessie. I am in love with you."

It was a wonderful statement to hear spoken aloud.

"So, it wasn't just a 'Jessie, I love you', as you were about to -?"

"I love you, Jessica Trelawny, and I love to make love to you."

She kissed him, "I love you too."

"You do?" and he suddenly looked like a little boy who had all his dreams come true at once.

"I do, I love you, Rob. And because I love you I need to know something. We need to be honest from the start."

"Of course," he held her hand.

"On the night of the opening," she squeezed his hand and felt awkward, "when you left here with Christy – did you sleep with her that night?"

He took a deep breath and then exhaled slowly, as if he felt queasy. He pursed his lips and stood up. At the kitchen counter he picked up a bottle of wine, "May I?"

She nodded, "I'll have one too."

He poured them each a glass and came back to the bed. As they sipped the delicious wine, he sat quietly. Then he said, "Yes, yes I did sleep with her."

"Ok," she nodded again, "at least I know for sure, now." She was deep in thought, he could see. "It's better to know," she spoke quietly, "I'm glad you told me."

"How did you know?"

"Christy took great delight in coming here to tell me herself. She told me you two were meant to be together, that you are a cheater and you play around, but she accepts that. After your nights of passion elsewhere, you always go home to her."

Rob put his head in his hands. Jess wondered if he was going to disclose everything to her. What had happened between them? What was the exchange like? How eager had he been? He had gone so far as to admit it. Would he tell her what had gone on?

"It's best to get it out into the open. I don't want there to be any secrets between us."

'Well now,' she thought, 'I have to listen to how he was with someone else – who hates me and all I stand for – on the opening night of my restaurant.'

"She persuaded me that you weren't interested in me. You had a life in London and a business that had nothing to do with me. She said you thought you were above us here."

Jess said nothing. She waited for him to give her the awful detail.

"She had me doubting myself, and you. After you told me you didn't want to see me – it was like nothing mattered to me. I saw you that evening. You looked so great and you're so talented. Everyone celebrated with you and you seemed to be fine. Getting on with your life."

"So, she convinced you I was a snob and wouldn't want to be with you?" she laughed slightly at the ridiculousness of the idea. She looked at him and considered how handsome and capable he was. 'How could I possibly think I was too good for him?'

"You really don't know me if you could think that," she was firm and honest.

"But I want to," he held her. "I feel mortified and stupid." "We can handle anything," she declared. "Any misunderstandings – we'll work through them. But we know, now, to believe each other and no one else. I will always be honest with you."

"And I will never cheat on you, never ever. Do you mind an idiot for a boyfriend?"

She kissed him. "You do know what the best thing about falling out is?"

"What's that?" he had a cheeky grin to die for.

"The angry make-up sex!" and she grabbed him and they fell onto the bed together.

Jess was not marking her territory, as such, but she had in the back of her mind never to let him think that he could have more fun elsewhere.

They were smiling and happy as they made love. She felt lucky, confident, and contented about her boyfriend, and her business, and her life right now.

Nothing could spoil it.

19 DESTRUCTION

Morning came.

Jess and Rob woke up slowly. After a good bottle of wine and some very intense and necessary make-up sex, they had slept very well.

Jess justified this in her mind because Duncan's team were on their way, she had no prep to do, and hair and make-up professionals who could work wonders on her. So, they slept in. Rob spooned against her. They kissed and snoozed and had a proper Sunday morning as a couple. They talked and found out more about each other.

Jess began to understand his character. Chemistry, passion, physical attraction – these aspects worked well between them. Effortlessly, seamlessly. She drew him out and he talked about his childhood. There had been happiness and unhappiness. She could sympathise with some of what he had been through. She had not experienced the death of a parent at a young age, but when Kristof left – it was a death of sorts.

Time stood still for Jess. Just for a little while Rob's strong, passionate body as he lay with her was a distraction from real life. She began to understand that it was a decision in itself to be with someone and not always think about pushing yourself and working harder.

Work smart.
Work careful.

Jess wanted it all. She wanted her restaurant and her this new love. And so, she decided to put everything else aside. No one would distract her now or make her feel bad about her ideas or her ambitions. Fully committed to her future, she decided she would spend time with Rob and allow for a mutually beneficial project with Duncan.

Snuggling into Rob's back, after fresh coffee, Jess breathed him in. She felt calm and happy.

An urgent knock at the Loft door.
Jess groaned, "Who can that be?" And she got up slowly, still fuggy. She had been so relaxed but she knew she had to wake up and pay attention. Rob, on the other hand, was up in an instant and answered the door.

Matty stood in the doorway. She was distraught.
"Oh, thank goodness you're here, Rob! Come quickly, both of you."

They all three clattered down the outside wooden steps. Jess, confused, pulled on her jumper and Rob – being Rob – was ready for action. At the door of the Loft's downstairs dining-room they halted. Matty stood in front of Jess.
"I don't think you should go in," her aunt said to her.
"What's happened?" she pushed past her aunt and into the dining-room.
"I came to open up this morning, before the journalists – and this is what it looked like."

Jess stood in the middle of the room, in shock. She looked around at the upturned tables, torn cushions, broken chairs, and the flour, ketchup, mustard, and paint daubed about. Profanities were scrawled across the table tops and on the walls.

"What the hell happened?" Rob looked around and went to Jess. He held her. Matty started to cry. The room was wrecked. There was nothing untouched by the vandalism.
"Who could have done this?" Matty sobbed.

Jess buried her face in Rob's chest, wanting to block out the sight of her pride and joy, her home, her father's home, unrecognisable. To make matters worse, at that moment Duncan and his entourage pulled up outside. With a clattering of heels in the courtyard and wafts of expensive fragrance they arrived at the door.

Duncan announced, "Darlings, this is Hesther – hair – and Gavin – make-up – Oh. My. God." His eyes were like saucers.

Gavin, make-up, leaned into the room over Duncan's shoulder, looked around and said, "Is this a bad time?"

Duncan stepped carefully over the debris towards Jess and Rob. "What happened, my darling?"

Jess raised her head from Rob's chest and looked him in the face. "Not *what – who*! Christy," she said quietly, "that's who, Christy." She headed out of the door.

"Oh, bloody hell," Rob followed her. He spoke to Matty over his shoulder, "Best call the police."

20 REFLECTION

Jess, with her stiff ankle, limped angrily down the High Street of Portlyon. She fumed as she aimed for the hill that led to Rob's house.

"Wait," he caught up with her and took her arm. "Please, wait."
"Is she back at your place? Is she there?"
"I don't know, but you're not steaming in there like this."
"Oh? Protecting her now, are you?"
"No! But what do you think you're going to do when you get there?"
"With my one good foot? I'm going to kick her arse," she said calmly.
Jess wrenched her arm away from him and continued on her way. But he persevered, "I'm not going to let you."
"*You're* not going to let *me*? Oh, nice try," and she continued on her way.
"At least let me drive you. It's a steep hill."

In silence, they drove up the hill towards his house. His family home was one of the large double-fronted, rambling, Victorian stone-built villas. There was enough space for Christy and Rob to have led separate lives under one roof.

Jess was first out of the Landrover. As she slammed the door of the vehicle she could not help but admire the beautiful, traditional house.
"I'll get the door," Rob raced past her up the pathway, "but I still think we should wait and find out if it was her first."
Jess turned to face him. "It was her, all right. There's a pattern here. When she came to the Loft – to *my* home – to warn me off you, she

105

started to break my stuff and tried to threaten me. I had to drag her out by her hair."

Rob paused, and then said, "Remind me not to get on your bad side."

He unlocked the front door and they walked into the tiled hallway.

"Christy," Rob called out cautiously.

The house was silent. They walked through the rooms together. Jess saw his home for the first time. Christy's presence, she knew, had kept him from welcoming her there. She saw how lovely it was and what his family home meant to him. Wooden floors, stained glass details, lots of old tiles. All of it was well-cared for and well-kept. His parents' possessions were still around and the family photographs neatly framed and displayed up the stairwell. Fallon at hockey practice. Rob and his father on board the 'Carrie-Ann'. Rob and Dan on the rugby team. And little Rob and Fallon with their mother, Caroline, happy and relaxed wearing wellington boots and carrying watering-cans in the garden.

As Jess walked through the house she calmed down. Suddenly, she saw the story of his life through this window into his family's history. They had built a home, full of spirit and love.

There was no sign of Christy as they walked through the downstairs rooms. Up the creaking wooden staircases and across landings. Into the room Christy occupied, drawers lay open and linens were tossed to one side on the bed. Jess looked around the room and then her foot kicked something that lay near the bed. It rolled away and she picked it up.

"Spray paint?" she held the can up for Rob to see. "She wasn't even bothered enough to hide it properly. And there's more under the bed."

But no sign of Christy.

"She must have been planning to do a runner for a while."

"She's cleared out. All her things are gone."

Jess sat down on the bed, holding the can of paint. She sighed as she looked around the room again.

"Well, you have a lovely home," she smiled but felt sad inside at the thought of everything she had recently built up being shattered so easily out of spite and jealousy.

Rob sat down beside her on the bed and put his arm around her. She tilted her head against his shoulder.

"What do I have to do to feel safe and happy?"

He turned to her and lifted her chin up to look into her face. "I love you. And I'm sorry. You've got me now, and we'll fix it."

"You don't need to apologise."

"I do. It's my fault Christy tried to attack you. I didn't realise she was so – disturbed."

"Crazy girls are supposed to be more exciting."

"Believe me, they aren't!"

"Am I enough for you?"

"I need you, Jessie, I really do." He kissed her gently and deeply. Then he rested his forehead against hers, and held her hand.

"Jessie," he spoke her pet-name quietly, "I only want you and to be happy and close to you. From the day I met you I had dreams about seeing you here in this house. I didn't imagine it like this, though! But I want you to know my home."

They kissed again.

Despite her sadness, she felt a stab of longing – to be here with him in the moment. She returned his kiss. He breathed hard, and took her face in his hands. He kissed her hungrily and deeply. His fingers found the buttons of her blouse and as he kissed her neck and down to her bosom he cupped one breast through her lace bra. She now wore the good underwear. He massaged gently with his hand, his thumb rubbing her nipple through the fabric. His other hand was knotted in her tousled hair, pulling her towards him. Their mouths strained together. He grew more insistent and she gasped and moaned – then stopped him.

"What, what is it?" his face looked a little desperate, even slightly panicked.

"Not here," she pressed her hands against his chest. "Show me where you sleep."

He grasped her hand and practically dragged her out of the room, across the landing, and along a corridor into a light, wood panelled room. There was a bay window that looked down onto the town and out towards Penlyon Cove. She could see the clifftop where they had met, where he had grabbed her, thinking he had to save her. She remembered the passion that had excited in her even then.

Rob's room had pale, painted floorboards and a limestone fireplace. A large, Victorian brass bed dominated the space. Laid across it was a beautifully crafted patchwork quilt. Jess held his hand, feeling a little awkward at first. She felt modest and shy all of a sudden.
"It's lovely in here," she looked at him.
"Lovelier now, with you here," he pulled her towards him, firmly, even a little roughly. She felt the urge to allow him to take control of her. She trusted him so much, the shadow of Christy in their lives dissolved quickly as their passion took over. He reached for her waist, his hands moving down to her buttocks, and pressed her against his body. Her arms wound around his neck and they moved together onto the bed. He started to remove her clothes again. Pulling at the fastening of her jeans. She arched her hips upwards to make it easier for him. First, her trousers, then her blouse, knickers, and finally her bra all strewn on the floor.

Spread naked on his bed, Jess sighed with pleasure as he slowly, deliberately, worked his mouth down her body. He pulled his clothes off as he did this. His desire for her was on show as he discarded his underwear. Then, quickly, he moved down between her legs and kissed her mound. He began to lick, slowly, and she grew flushed and swollen. She gasped and moved against his mouth, naturally, following her instincts for gaining pleasure from him. This was a new experience for her.

Her sex-life until Rob had been fun, but conventional. It had given her pleasure, but it was vanilla. Before Rob, no man had ever gone down on her. She was partly astonished, partly embarrassed, and overwhelmingly ecstatic with the bliss of it. Pure pleasure for her. She panted, panicking a little, and came hard, spasming. He held her tightly, keeping his tongue close to her clitoris. She shuddered with her intense orgasm. It felt to her as though he was making this their place. So intimate, so passionate, here together in a world of their own.

He kissed his way up her body and held her. They kissed and she tasted herself as his tongue moved into her mouth.
"Are you ready?" he breathed.
'Yes. I want you so much."
He lifted her up slightly, and she was unsure what he was doing at first. With a shudder of desire, she realised he wanted her on her hands and knees. He positioned himself behind her and she felt his hardness against her buttocks. He stroked the tip of his penis between them, and she trembled, breathing hard. His fingers moved and stroked, touched, and rubbed the lips of her vagina, easing them open. He rocked against her and she cried out with pleasure as he pushed into her.
"Are you ok?" she heard him ask, his voice deep with desire.
"Yes, yes," she spoke urgently, "please, don't stop."

Rob reached forwards and rubbed one of her breasts as his hips rocked against her. It felt painful at first, undeniably painful. All she could do was cry out with a pain that immediately evaporated into the most intense pleasure she had ever felt. She could only call out his name and almost collapse with the effect of it. She was afraid of what she was feeling.

Jess looked around at him and saw the pure lust in his eyes. A powerful expression of complete desire overwhelmed his face. She felt a sense of pure joy – that she could raise such feelings in him. She looked back and suddenly caught sight of the two of them in a mirror near the fireplace. They both felt her spasm in response to the sight of their love-making.
"Oh God!" she heard him exclaim.
She could not resist now, mesmerised. She turned back slightly towards the mirror. He saw then – saw both of them – too. They

locked eyes as their passion mounted and gazed at one another. She took in the whole sight of him, his strength as he thrust, the irresistible movement of his hips. He pounded into her, his hands clamped to her hips and buttocks. Her breasts bounced rhythmically beneath her. She felt free. She felt complete openness. She could ask him anything now to fulfil her pleasures, she knew, and he would meet it. His pleasure arose from her pleasure.

"Harder," she gasped, "harder!'

All she could think about now was the centre of her being and the sensations that were exploding inside her. They did not lose eye contact in the mirror, both smiled, as he gripped her. She saw her face flushed with pleasure, and he lost all control. With a loud grunt and a grimace of passion he came inside her. He shuddered and collapsed against her. He held her tight, earnestly kissed her back and her buttocks.

Rob reached for her, and, wordlessly he covered them both with the quilt. He held her, they nestled, curled up against each other. Jess cleared her mind. After what they had just shared she did not want to think about Christy being here with him. Rob seemed to read her mind, "It wasn't in here. She was never in here."
Jess rolled over to face him and rested her chin on his firm chest. She looked up at him, with his finely arched dark brows and stubbly chin, his dark, clear eyes and weathered complexion. She smiled at him.
"I have no fears now, no worries. I love you, that's what matters."
"I love you too," he stroked the tip of her nose and gazed into her pale, lilac eyes. "Oh, and another thing. After today – I'm really scared of you!"
"As you should be!"

Rob and Jess showered together. They kissed as the warm water soaked their bodies. He towel-dried her curls as she sat on the bed, wearing his warm robe. He kissed the top of her head and the unruly mass of silky, honey-blonde hair. They dressed and Rob collected his tool box and belt, in order to see what needed to be fixed when he got back to the restaurant. They strolled together down the hill back to the Loft, hand in hand.

"I will have to close indefinitely until I can fix all the damage and clean-up," she contemplated as they walked, "and I can kiss goodbye to having a feature with Duncan in 'What's Hot?'."
He put his arm around her. "You've got me. And Fallon, Lyla, and Matty – we're family now."
They stopped just before the turning into Sailmaker's Yard.
"Really? Family?"
"If you'll have us? You're my family and I'm yours."
They put their foreheads together.

Jess closed her eyes as the tears welled in them. She felt herself give a slight sob that she quickly swallowed.
"You're a sensitive soul, aren't you? You can let it out with me." He smiled and kissed her kindly.
Jess took a deep breath to brace herself for what confronted her around the corner. She walked into the yard with him, a united front to deal with anything Christy's revenge had to throw at them.

An unexpected sight met her eyes.

21 INSPIRATION

Jess stopped in the Yard, uncertain of what she was looking at.

The tables from the dining-room were arranged around and some of the damaged chairs surrounded them. Buckets of warm, soapy water and mops were stood about. Lyla and Matty called out to one another from inside the dining-room.
Music played. There was almost a party atmosphere.

Gavin – make-up – and Hesther – hair – wiped down the tables, scrubbing off paint and the caked-on flour.
Gavin looked up from his work with a grin, "Did you get the bitch?"
"What's going on here?" Jess walked up to them. "What are you doing?"
"All hands to the pumps," Hesther was gingerly buffing a tile. "Those two in there, is that your aunt? They decided to get on with it."
"Thank you, thank you both," Jess stammered. She walked past them into the dining-room as Duncan arrived with a tray of hot drinks.
"There are some very agreeable people around here. They couldn't do enough when I told them about our predicament. I've got skinny caps and even soy lattes. Jessica, baby!" He air-kissed in her direction as she walked inside.
"Did you?" Gavin called out to her, he turned around to Rob, "Did she get her?"
Rob shook his head, "She was long gone."
"Shame. The plot thickens," he laughed. "And you," he held out a hand to Rob, "must be the boyfriend? The rock?"

"Yes, Rob. How do you do?"

"Gavin. Looks like you've come prepared." Gavin eyed Rob's toolbelt approvingly.

"Where shall I start?" Rob asked.

"Oh darling – that's a loaded question!" Hesther laughed and patted him on the chest.

"Ahem," Jess was at the door, arms folded.

"Gotta go," Rob looked across at her and shrugged to Hesther, "the boss needs me."

"Pity," the hairstylist replied.

Jess took his arm. Now it was her turn to be proprietorial.

Jess's fears and sadness had been somewhat allayed, once she had seen the progress that Matty and Lyla had made. The two loyal helpers had cleaned the ketchup and gunk off the walls and placed any broken furniture on one side. Rob got to work on this, gluing and screwing, pegging struts that had been kicked in. Luckily, the damage Christy had done was superficial, she was not so strong as to do any lasting harm.

Sadly, though, Lyla was having less luck with the graffiti across the walls.

"It's just not budging at all," she scrubbed at the stubborn paint with detergent. Matty stood alongside her with some stronger cleaning spray.

"Not much luck with this one, either."

They tried their best to rid one of the walls from the words scrawled in red spray paint: 'Fucking Bitch'.

Duncan looked on with the coffees. He considered the wall.

"I'm going to have to completely paint it over," Jess felt despondent. She had wanted to avoid the cost of redecoration. "And I don't want to use strong chemical cleaners in here."

Duncan put his cup down, decisively. "Leave it," he said. "I think we can use this."

Jess looked sideways at him.

"Trust me," he reassured her, "*and* we'll help with the clean-up costs afterwards. I've got a great idea for the shoot."

"Seriously? With it looking like this?"

"I know what I'm talking about. Come on, we've got work to do."

The day turned into an even more strange and interesting one. By the end of it, Jess realised, she had not thought about Christy's act of revenge at all. Instead, she, Matty, and Lyla had been treated and pampered by Gavin and Hesther, while Duncan and the photographer, Maia, and her assistant fixed up the set and lit everything.

Duncan's brainwave was to use the trashed, vandalised dining-room as an ironic backdrop.

Jess was photographed sitting serenely in chef's whites, flanked by the perfectly groomed Matty and Lyla, in the midst of flung condiments and spray-painted walls. The three of them looked confidently and archly into the camera. Jess, with arms folded, adopted the pose that Duncan insisted was the classic 'celebrity' chef image.

Rob looked on, proudly, from the side-lines as Jess had her time in the sun. Gavin touched up her lips and cheeks under the lights. The make-up artist smirked wickedly and looked over at Rob whilst he applied the brush.
"You've got yourself a real smitten kitten there, haven't you?"
"Is it that obvious?" Jess blushed under her perfectly airbrushed coating of make-up.
"Oh please! Those shoulders, that tool-belt – to die for!"
"He's a fisherman too, and the skipper of the lifeboat crew."
Gavin rolled his eyes and groaned, "It gets worse, a total babe *and* a hero!"
"He actually saved me."
"What?"
"I fell and slid down the cliff face at the cove and he rescued me."
Gavin paused, lip-brush in the air, and then hugged her. "You are my patron saint. You're proof that heaven *is* a place on earth, Belinda Carlisle."
Maia took off-duty behind-the-scenes shots and caught Jess's gleeful reaction to this comment, whilst Rob looked on in the background.

After a fruitful and strange day, Lyla and Matty, Rob and Jess sat together on the deck and shared a bottle of wine.

"*That*," Matty breathed a sigh, "was a truly bizarre day."

"Have you heard anything from the police.?"

"They will 'look into it'," Jess shrugged and naturally, easily, rested her aching foot in Rob's lap. In the chill evening sunlight, they sat, relaxed and talking.

Lyla topped up her drink, "More importantly, when will the article come out?"

"Online from next Saturday," Jess yawned, "I'm too tired to think about anything else now."

Rob rubbed her ankle.

Lyla and Matty smiled at one another as they observed Rob's devotion. As soon as they had finished their drinks they made their exit.

"Come on, we've got a long day ahead of us, tidying and repainting. Good night." Matty kissed her niece's forehead.

"Night, Aunty."

The two women made their way out of Sailmaker's Yard in the early December twilight. They glanced back up at the Loft and saw Jess now curled up on Rob's lap, wrapped in a fleece blanket. He cradled her in his arms and stroked her hair gently.

"That's something special, right there," Lyla nodded sagely.

"You're not wrong," Matty waved them goodnight.

22 INFLUENCES

Jess sat at her desk in the Loft. Another bright, cold morning in Portlyon. Seagulls keened and shrieked outside the windows. She worked hard on the orders and menus every day. Her mission for the restaurant was the creation of a signature style, something distinctive and local. Something to be proud of.

Deep in thought about fennel and mushrooms for Fallon and Lyla's wedding party, she was disturbed by her phone ringing. She did not recognise the number though, London calling.

"Hello, is that Jessica?" an unfamiliar voice spoke.
"Yes, who is this?"
"It's Hugo, how are you?"

Jess's mind raced back to her father's funeral, months before. Hugo and his brother, Jeremy, her half-brothers. Kristof's sons from his first marriage.
"Hugo?" she could not hide the surprise in her voice. "I'm well, thank you." She was bewildered. As a girl she had met him twice and then for a third time at the funeral. This was the first time for any conversation between them.
"I saw the article. I wanted to congratulate you on the success of your new restaurant."
Jess felt slightly suspicious, guarded. Hugo's tone was friendly and brisk.

116

"I was thinking, it's about time we caught up with what you're doing. It sounds very exciting – what you're doing there at the Loft. Father made the right choice in leaving you the property."

This came with the insinuation, Jess thought, that there had been conversations about it being the wrong choice.

Later on, and still feeling indecisive, Jess called her mother.

"Hello, darling!" there was a sense of anticipation and excitement in Lizbeth's voice.

"Hugo called me."

"I *know!*" Her mother was gleeful on the end of the line. "He called me and I gave him your number. Exciting isn't it?"

Jess was even more wary. Of all the people her mother could have been excited about, her half-brother was not someone she would have thought of.

"This could be a *real* game-changer, you should meet him."

For the first time in months, Jess made her way into Covent Garden. She realised that she did not miss London. At least, not living and working there. However, the Christmas lights and decorations were up in the streets and shops. There were the sounds of carols piped into the public spaces. Smells of chestnuts and honied crepes drifted from the array of food-stalls as she walked up from the tube station.

She strolled through the market and purchased a bag of sweet chestnuts from a vendor. She licked the sweetness off her fingers and browsed the shop windows. She had a little time until her meeting with Hugo. At one of the bijou shops, she paused, then went in. After a few minutes, she emerged with a small jeweller's bag. Then, onwards to the restaurant, not far from her old place of work at The Centre. She saw old familiar sights.

When she walked into the small, smart bistro Hugo greeted her and led her to the table where another man already sat. He stood up to greet Jess.

"This is Sinclair, Sinclair Brookes. He's an old friend of mine," Hugo explained. "Sinclair is an investor, he works in hedge fund management."

117

"I am always on the look-out for a new project to broaden my portfolio. Your establishment, Miss Trelawny, is quite an exciting prospect."

There had been a time, when she lived in London that Jess would feel mousy and shy in the company of these well-groomed and expensively tailored men. To Jess's amusement, Hugo took on the role of elder brother. He portrayed a protective fraternalism with awkwardness and embarrassment. Clearly, he had not disclosed to Sinclair the extent, or lack of it, of his relationship with Jess. She felt at ease, however. She did not feel gratitude for being allowed into the conversation. Their demeanour and charm told her how much they wanted her attention. Starting her own business and meeting Rob had helped Jess's confidence to soar. So, in many ways, she now felt equal to these men, who once she would have felt privileged to serve from the kitchen.

Hugo started to scrutinise the menu, and Sinclair made interested noises. The waiter came up to the table.
"Gentlemen," Jess spoke politely, "will you allow me to order for you?"
Both looked a little surprised and then recognised that they were in the company of a woman who knew what she was talking about. In fact, her expertise was the very reason they were there. In flawless French, Jess made a discriminating selection and worked from the waiter's recommendations for the specials and the wine.

During the impressive lunch, the kitchen and waiting staff could not do enough for them. The word had gone around that Jess Trelawny was in, and they wanted to make sure she felt welcome. Hugo, clearly gratified with the results of his networking, disclosed his plan to his half-sister. He had a new-found interest in her but he acted as though they were close family from way back. She thought, 'what the heck?' And played along. Sinclair was looking to invest and saw The Sailmaker's Loft as a great opportunity. Her interview had been picked up by a national Sunday newspaper. Ripples had moved outwards after that. The striking image, the great endorsements, and the edgy contrasts. The graffiti, with the insults and profanity, caused a stir. Jess came across as hard-working and creative and someone, as Sinclair described in a polite fashion, 'who doesn't take nonsense from anyone'.

Jess did not let on about anything to do with the real story and Christy's vandalism of the restaurant. She thought that it might make her personal life sound too messy and in danger of compromising any investment. She let them believe that the whole shoot had been part of a publicity strategy.

Before she left for London, the night before, Jess and Rob had talked when he saw her off at the station.
"Don't have your head turned in the big city," he joked and kissed her on the nose. He held her close before she boarded, however, to just seal in her mind how London could not offer her what she had in Portlyon. Time dragged for her on the journey and as she navigated London.

Now that she was mixing with Hugo and Sinclair, she felt distracted enough, from missing the Loft and Rob.
"I want to get to know you better," Sinclair was saying and raised his glass to Jess, "will you come to my headquarters tomorrow and we can discuss things?"
Jess looked at Hugo, who nodded his approval and then back to Sinclair.
"Your HQ?"
"On Carnegie Square, off Queensway. We'll send a car for you in the morning."

Later that evening, Jess sat in her mother's kitchen and listened to Lizbeth's excitement.
"You could branch out into all sorts of areas, if Hugo and Sinclair decide to invest in you. You could create cookware, write books, have endorsements of all kinds."
Jess sat opposite Alastair who smiled indulgently at Lizbeth, in full flow. She was passionate about what she saw as her daughter's impending 'success'.

119

"And just think," Lizbeth ignored her food whilst her imagination ran on, "there could be television and personal appearances. You know, the food festival and literature circuit? It's all about getting your name on the poster for promotions and events."

Alastair smiled, "And you never know, Jess, you might even get the chance to do some cooking."

Lizbeth smacked him on the arm, playfully.

"I think Jess can make the right decisions for her and her business, love."

"Of course – of course – you do whatever you want to, darling. Although, I will say one thing – corporates! Corporate events – once you have a name, businesses will pay huge one-off fees to have your personal services."

Jess stayed quiet during this inundation. She genuinely appreciated her mother's enthusiasm and excitement, but had heard something from Lizbeth that disturbed her, or at least make her question why she was there. She had talked about Jess's possible *future* success.

Jess considered what she did *now*, and how her life was moving forward, to be a success. She was going in the right direction. She was happy with the certainty of Rob's feelings. All doubts about them were dispelled for her and the restaurant was working out. They had rolled on quietly from week to week, started to break even, and were now turning a small profit.

Despite the late hour, Jess excused herself and went into the quiet sitting room. She called Rob, wanting to hear his voice. A text was not enough.

She heard him and was instantly comforted. She felt reassured as she listened to his sleepy Cornish drawl and longed to be with him.

"Only agree to what you want," he said with a yawn. "You know what's best for you and your business."

She felt the distance from him, his voice was small but his words were huge and filled her heart.

"How is your mother?"

"She's fine."

"Does she disapprove of me yet?" she returned his laugh.

"Alastair sends his best."
"And I to him. Do you know when you're coming home? The bed is way too empty." She heard him stretching. "I miss you."
"I miss you too. I'm coming home soon."
"Is this home now? Not London anymore?"
"I love you," Jess smiled, "and home is wherever you are."
"I love you too. Oh – gotta go – someone's at the door, I think," and he rang off.

Silence. She felt lonely, and also something else. An uneasiness. Jess made a resolution there and then. She called a cab.

"I don't see why you can't stay put here – until tomorrow. You'll be on the train overnight. It will be so uncomfortable."
Jess was putting her few things in her backpack, whilst her mother stood by.
"I'll nap on the train."
Lizbeth gasped, "What about Hugo and Sinclair? You were supposed to meet them to talk business. I can't believe you're walking away from this."
Jess paused and smiled at her, "It's not the end. It's just the beginning. There's time enough to talk to them about what might happen. I know what I want for my life right now, and I want that life to start as soon as possible.
"And what you want is this Rob?"
Jess smiled, "It's my place in Portlyon, on my terms, and yes, it's Rob too."

Lizbeth hugged her tightly.
"Don't make the same mistake I made," she was feeling weepy and a little tipsy. "You're my beautiful, brave girl and I'm worried for you."
"I know, and I'm glad you are. You've got my back and whatever happens, I know you're here for me."
"It's not too big a risk though? I don't want you to get your heart broken.
"It's a risk – everything's a risk – but it's one I'm willing to take."
"And you *will* call Hugo and Sinclair?"

"I'll call them, and arrange a new meeting. I just want to go home now."

The sound of the cab – a horn outside.

"Goodbye," she kissed her mother. Alastair enveloped her in one of his bear hugs.

"Take care, love, and be happy," he winked at her.

"I'll try," and she was out of the door and into the night for the express to the West Country from Paddington.

23 RETURN TO PORTLYON

Jess arrived at the small Portlyon railway station at around four-thirty in the morning. The express had taken her on the mainline into Cornwall and then she changed trains to complete the long, winding journey into the winter dawn along the coast. It called at every out of the way place and she was again reminded of childhood holidays.

When she alighted at Portlyon there was a feathery night-time hoar frost everywhere. The air was crisp and clear. She felt happy to be there, truly comfortable and at home. With no chance of a cab she was happy to walk and set off through the town towards the hill road up to Rob's house. She thought, excitedly, how surprised he would be at her arrival and could hardly wait to curl up in the soft comfort of his arms under the warm patchwork quilt.

The town slept. Under a blanket of frosting she had never known anything so quiet. Every surface was dusted with crystals. Leaves and branches glistened. Jess tramped up the hill, her breath clouded in the night air. The sound of her footsteps on the cobbled street was the only sound. Christmas lights twinkled around doorways and window frames.

As she turned the corner that led towards the narrow lane up to the clifftop, she heard the wash of breaking waves along the shore of Penlyon Cove below. The soft sounds travelled in the chill air. She looked up the hill, towards Rob's house, and something caught her eye. She noticed a change in colour behind the rooftops of the cottages along the lane. An unexpected smell met her nostrils. Frost and cold mixed with ash and heat.

Jess started to run, pulling out her mobile phone as she did, cold terror clutched at her heart.

The heat from the fire that consumed the ground floor of Rob's clifftop villa drove her back when she reached it. The cold, dark of the night was melted by the bright flames gushing and flickering from the hallway and front living-room windows. The glass cracked crazily, buckled, and gave way as the flames licked the curtains.

She shouted above the flames as loud as she could, "Rob, Rob!" The smoke was stifling. Jess tied a cotton t-shirt from her pack around her mouth and nose and with her hood up she pushed aside the front door and battled her way into the hall. She called out for Rob again. She had no way of knowing whether he was there or not but she knew she had to risk it, just in case. She also knew that calling for the fire service would take too long and they could not get the fire engine up the narrow lane to the house. The disadvantage of living in a clifftop dwelling.

The rescuer could not be rescued, unless she took the initiative.

Obstacles barred her way up the stairs. Wooden chairs hampered her progress, placed there deliberately, there could be no other explanation. But she could not think about that now. Smoke filled the upstairs. That was the big problem, worse than the flames.

She heard sirens in the distance. Someone had alerted the emergency teams.

Coughing, she found the door to Rob's bedroom. She rattled the handle. It was locked. She pounded on it and called his name again. She looked around frantically. The house seemed eerily still above the flames. They were not spreading up there yet, but the smoke and the heat were.

From within the bedroom, she heard a noise, a scuffling and coughing. She called out again, "Rob? Rob? Can you make it to the door? I can't get it open."

124

She heard some more movement and coughing and then she saw the handle rattle.

"It's locked," she heard his hoarse, fuddled voice on the other side. He put his weight against it but the sturdy Victorian lock held fast.

"Have you got the key?"

"I can't see it anywhere," he sounded confused.

"I'll be as quick as I can, I'm coming back."

Jess braced herself to go downstairs into the hall again. The seconds ticked by agonisingly. It felt like hours as she searched for something – anything – she could use on the door. She managed to return through the smoke and rising flames, up the stairs with a large, brass pot that had been the umbrella stand.

"Stand back," she shouted at the door and brought the pot down on the lock. Once, twice, three times and a hard kick with all her strength. Smoke billowed from out of the room. The beautiful, pale, panelled walls were blackened and sooty. Rob was slumped on the floor by the bed, the patchwork quilt partially covering him. She reached out to him and held his hand. His eyes looked strange and she realised that something must have happened to make him this confused. A head injury?

Jess scooped an arm around him and helped him to his feet. She turned with him, hobbling, back to the stairs but with a roar, the flames confronted them. The hallway and stairs were on fire and the flames beat them back into the bedroom. She helped Rob onto the bed and secured the door. She wet some towels in the bedroom sink and wedged them along the bottom of the door. Then she looked around the room with the little time she had bought them. Now, however, she was at a loss as to what to do.

'Think, think, Jess,' she said to herself.

Rob did not look good. He was woozy, coughing, disoriented. She saw the paint on the inside of the door begin to blister, crack, and darken. The floorboards felt hot.

She picked up a chair and smashed it through the bay window. Cold air rushed in allowing her to breathe more freely for a few moments. She broke the frame and pushed the glass out.

"Come on," she hooked an arm around Rob and helped him off the bed, "my turn to help you."

They staggered over to the window and she looked down. To her eternal relief, she saw a collection of figures in neon yellow jackets, lit by the flames. Smoke and steam filled the air, blue lights flickered off the frost down the hill. The top of a ladder thumped onto the window sill. Voices called out to Jess. She leaned Rob against the wall and called down.

"He's hurt," she indicated Rob, "he needs to get out first."

The firefighters took charge. Two of them manoeuvred Rob to the window whilst Jess watched anxiously. She did not allow herself to feel any relief until he was clear of the building and the ladder. When she reached the foot of the ladder they had already strapped him onto a trolley and paramedics secured some insulated blankets over him. He was struggling and protesting.

"Where's Jessie, is she ok?"

The medic calmed him down. Hoses were unravelled to start dousing the blaze.

"She's here, she fine. Now lie still."

Jess was at his side. His soot-marked face glistened in the flames. She had never before loved anyone as much as she loved Rob right there and then. His dark brows were knitted in concern and he coughed harshly as she clasped his hand.

"Jessie," he tried to turn towards her but they had him immobilised in a neck brace.

"I'm here, be still," she cautioned, and smoothed the tousled hair on his damp forehead. The ambulance backed up the lane. Jess caught sight of Fallon and Matty – consternation deeply etched on their faces – and then she was rapidly gathered up into the ambulance alongside Rob.

A paramedic planted an oxygen mask on his face to ease his breathing, so he could say nothing else. Jess was wrapped in a

blanket and secured into the back of the vehicle. He reached across
and held her hand as they pulled away, lights and sirens blaring.

24 PROTECTION

Jess stirred in the uncomfortable chair with its vinyl cover. She pulled the thin blanket around her shoulder and slowly opened her eyes.

Across from her, in the hospital bed, Rob lay still. His breathing more peaceful and easier now. A drip-stand stood nearby, the tube fed into the cannula on the back of his hand. There was no need for oxygen now, just fluids. He had received treatment in time, before the smoke inhalation was too severe. Jess had got him out in time. What was harder to deal with was the concussion. It was that, not the smoke, that had caused such disorientation.
"Did he strike his head?" the doctor had asked her.
"I don't know, not when I was there."

She moved her chair quietly, closer to the bed and took his hand. He stirred slightly but remained asleep. No more wheezing or gasping for breath, she could tell in the stillness of the room, but they were both still soot-stained. She squeezed his hand on an impulse and kissed it.

Rob's brow furrowed. The winter light filtered in through the blinds against the window.
"Jessie," his dry voice spoke her name clearly.
"I'm here, I'm here."
She had insisted on remaining with him. The ward staff were fine with that. If she slept in the chair next to him it saved on a bed.

Rob tried to moisten his lips. Jess reached for the cup of water on the table and helped him to drink. He quenched his thirst gratefully. "Thank you," he murmured and looked at her lovingly. "Thank you – for everything."
"I'm just returning the favour."
She smiled and went to kiss him gently on the forehead. With an unexpected burst of strength his hand moved around her waist and he pulled her towards him. She steadied herself against the pillow and their lips met in a passionate kiss. He knitted the fingers of one hand in her messy curls. When she pulled away they smiled softly at one another.
"Feeling better?"
"I am now," and he managed a small, croaky laugh.

The nurse bustled in, "Good, good." She helped him to sit up. "You're one lucky fellow, considering," she chirruped in her Cornish burr. She adjusted and checked the drip and took his pulse and temperature. "Any pain?"
He shook his head.
"Good. You'll be able to have some visitors soon," at this she gestured to the corridor. "We're overwhelmed with flowers and messages, but we can't bring the gifts onto the ward. There's a pile of them out there."

All of Portlyon wished them well. There were voicemails from Lizbeth and enormous bouquets from Hugo, Sinclair, and Duncan too, with an added video message on her phone showing him flanked by an anguished Gavin and Hesther.

But soon, Jess could take Rob home, to the Loft.

Once inside, she made him some tea and got him settled.
"I could get used to this," he joked and took her hand gently. He kissed it and pulled her down to the bed beside him.
"We've got to go easy, you've had a head injury."
She helped him to rest on the pillows. He still had dizzy spells.
They did not yet speak about the facts that lay before them. Christy must be the culprit. She had kept the keys to the house, and the one

to Rob's room. She let herself in, that was the noise Rob heard when he was on the call to Jess, and assaulted him. Whilst he was unconscious, she locked him in his bedroom and set obstacles on the stairs and in the hallway. She set a fire in the downstairs room. Vengeful, certainly. Murderous, almost. Deranged, probably. All this raced through Jess's mind. She felt sick to her stomach.

Rob had not mentioned how he felt about it. He had been very tactile with Jess, holding her hand, embracing her, kissing her at every opportunity since they had left the hospital. It was as if he was reassuring himself and comforting them both with touch and intimacy.

The doctor and the police agreed he had been the victim of a blunt force head injury. Everything pointed to Christy. The search was on to track her down. Everyone was shocked that the woman could bear such a jealous grudge. Jess was not shocked. She had seen the look in Christy's eye that day in her home. Spite had turned to jealousy and revenge. A woman on the brink. A case of, 'If I can't have him, no one can.'

Police officers were assigned to The Loft and to the Portlyon area to make sure that she did not get close to Jess and Rob. Jess stood on the deck and saw the patrol car parked down the street. She sensed that Rob was feeling pain and guilt. Pain at the danger that might face them both again and guilt that he had introduced such turmoil into Jess's life.

Where *was* Christy? That was the question. She had been so slippery. She vanished after the vandalism of the restaurant, leaving them to think that she had left for good after such a petty act, as if she had satisfied her desire for revenge. Jess had to admit that she had experienced a gut feeling that Christy would be back. She knew that it would not be enough for her just to inconvenience Jess by trashing her restaurant. But she could never have imagined she would take it so far.

Rob joined her on deck.

"I'm afraid I provoked her," she admitted to Rob.

He kissed her and held her tight as they stood there together.

"Anything she does is her responsibility. I should never have let her stay on. It's nothing to do with you."

They looked out towards the sea and across the town. The painful remains of Rob's family home sat on the clifftop. Half of the house was gone. Charred timbers sat visible in the cold, white morning. Some wafts of smoke still rose and water dripped and glistened off the debris.

Sadness overwhelmed Jess, thinking about Rob and all his family possessions. The photos that had lined the staircase were gone. The trinkets and ornaments blackened or destroyed. Then, she remembered something.

"Wait here," and she went back into the Loft and found her backpack. It had been dropped off at the hospital by Matty, who had the presence of mind to retrieve it at the scene of the fire. It smelt of smoke, as did her hair and all her clothes. Jess rummaged inside it. She was back outside within moments to Rob. She clasped the little package she had purchased from the small shop in Covent Garden.

"A gift, for me?"

"It's only small, but it will remind you – of us, I suppose!"

He unwrapped the box and took out two matching gold chains. On each one was a clasp and hook that held a single, ordinary shirt button. Rob looked at them curiously.

"What's this?"

Jess fixed one of the chains around his neck.

"Don't you recognise two of your old shirt buttons?"

He fixed the other chain around her neck.

"My shirt buttons?" and then the realisation hit him. "You mean these are from – no way?! You little vixen!"

She nodded, "A memento of the first time we managed an uninterrupted date."

"You found my buttons?"

"Actually, my Aunt Mathilde picked them up, without knowing what they were or where they came from. She put them away in her button box. I stole them."

He shook his head and laughed. "I love you so much."

They held each other. His arms protected her from the wintry sea breeze.

25 DISCOVERY

A face appeared through the winter rain. The drumming of drops on the windows of the Loft turned into a scratching at the shutters. Jess walked towards the window. The gale howled around the building.

"Who's there? Who's out there?" She walked barefoot on the painted floorboards. An odd feeling accompanied each step. She shuddered. Someone was out there in the cold storm.

A face through the winter rain.
Matted, drenched hair, pale skin. Jess blinked and looked closer. She pulled back suddenly.
Christy!
The woman's seething face pressed against the glass, dark eyes circled with pain. The sound of the glass shattering and a hand grabbed Jess's wrist. Bloodied fingers gripped hers, twisting her arm. Her breathing was ragged and she cried out.

"Jessie. Jessie. Jessica."

She opened her eyes and found she was lying in Rob's bed, in his room. Confused, she sat up, she thought she had heard his voice. Flames began to lick around the bed and consume the patchwork cover. The walls blackened around her. The window was gone and the night air rushed in upon her, making her gasp.

"Jessie, Jessie!" Rob's voice broke through into her waking dream. "You were having a nightmare."

Her breathing settled and she blinked rapidly and looked around the safety of the Loft. She was home, in bed, Rob held her. She buried her face in his shoulder.

"You didn't burn," there was a sob in her voice. "You didn't burn, you're safe and you didn't burn."

His lovely face looked down into hers.

"Christy made one fatal mistake," he smiled.

"What's that?" she sniffed.

"She hit me on the head."

Jess ran her fingers through his thick hair, carefully avoiding the dressing over his wound. "It's a handsome head," she looked at him. The trembling and breathlessness of her nightmare was soon replaced with the tremulous, gentle delight of making love. Slow and steady, beneath the night-time rain that fell on the skylight above them they took each other into tender ecstasies.

"Jessie, Jessie, I love you," he breathed as his orgasm overwhelmed him. She was on top, back arched and head thrown upwards. Her curls cascaded across her shoulders. Rob grasped her breasts, then her buttocks, in his passion until she collapsed onto him.

Afterwards, they held each other and talked, softly, into the breaking dawn as the rain fell. She felt healed of her nightmare. They did not want to create too much noise, with a church-like restraint, so as not to break the sacred spell they had conjured in their private space.

Rob cradled her against his chest, and they knitted their fingers together and spoke about their childhoods and the snippets they recalled of one another during summers in Portlyon.

"You used to sing a lot," he remembered, "and do dance numbers! How come you don't dance anymore?"

"How do you know I don't dance? I might do it in the privacy of my own home, in my undies!"

"Now that, I want to see!"

"What about your overalls? I remember the lovely way they used to drape off your shoulder. So skinny!" she laughed. He breathed in and flexed his muscles. "But you have filled out, very nicely, I approve."

Soon, the huge task of recreating her downstairs dining-room confronted Jess. A few days after Rob left hospital she felt confident to leave him resting. She stood at the entrance of her dining-room. The tables were stacked and the chairs turned around. It looked like the skeleton of a dining-room.

Jess rolled up her sleeves, and set to work. The challenge she faced was to take the graffiti off the walls without damaging the stone. It had made sense to use it for the photoshoot, but now, she thought, the time had come to reinstate the former ambience and make it her place again. She would put her stamp on it.

So, painting it in a traditional lime wash was the solution. She had ordered some new print copies of her father's posters in order to cover the defaced ones. She spread out some cloths and covered the furniture. With the lime mix in a bucket she began to apply it to the stone. It was a time-consuming and chilly chore. The lime dripped down her arm, but it spread quite easily on the surface and the coverage was good. She lit the stove and warmed her hands part way through the process, to try and bring her circulation back. She stood before the stove and contemplated what more she had to do, rubbing her nose and peeling off her rubber gloves. Then, she saw something strange.

26 GHOSTS

Two of the bricks at the side of the hearth appeared to be loose. The mortar in between was dry and crumbly. Where the bricks had fallen against one another, there was a hollow space. Jess recalled what Rob had said, that he had repointed the brickwork for Kristof as part of the maintenance on the Loft before her father left for France. Because the stove had been regularly lit over the past few months moisture had been drawn out of the brickwork for the first time in over a decade.

Jess peered closely at the gap. She tried to wriggle a couple of fingers in between the bricks. She was not sure that there should be a cavity there and dreaded the thought of a major overhaul of the chimney structure. Her pessimistic self immediately went to that. She gingerly prised one of the bricks away. It happened quite easily. The mortar crumbled and the brick above teetered so she slid that one out too. Curious, she peeped into the cavity, warm air emanated from it. A dry space beside the hearth. She could just about make something out in the dark. The cavity was not empty.

Rob dozed lightly in the warm bed upstairs in the studio. He wondered when Jess might be back to wriggle into bed with him.

She appeared, covered with spatters of lime wash, and shook him awake.
"Quick, come quick. I've got something to show you. Put your trousers on."
"Can't we stay put here?"
She kissed him quickly on the nose, "Time for that later."

Downstairs, the tables were arranged, and laid out on them was a curious collection. An array of sketchbooks and paintings. Paintings on canvasses, unrolled, displaying their vibrant colours.

"I found them," Jess said proudly, "beside the hearth, hidden in a cavity in the wall. Look." She picked up one of a series of hardback sketchbooks. The covers were dusty with age, but perfectly intact. She opened it for him to look and carefully turned the pages. "They are all full, cover to cover, with drawings. People on the beach, sailing boats, and children playing, building sandcastles."

Rob walked around the tables, taking it all in, as Jess spoke.

"And everything, the paintings and all the sketches, they're all by my father. But it's unlike anything of his I have ever seen before. He *never* produced work with people for subjects. That's his signature, though. And his style is unmistakable."

Life in Portlyon and days outs at Penlyon Cove were on show in lavish, living images. The narrow streets and colourful shop-fronts. Sun-burnt children running past in shorts, t-shirts, striped and multi-coloured, gulls above and cheerful flags flying. By far the most frequent subject was a little tousle-headed girl. She ate ice-cream, climbed on rocks, crouched beside rockpools armed with a net, and bucket and spade. Light bounced off her pale curls in a vibrant, stylised fashion. Even with the impressionistic style of thickly applied paint the identity of the girl was in no doubt.

"It's you, Jessie, it's all you," Rob put an arm around her shoulder and her head rested on him, strong and comforting.

Spread out before them was Jess's timespan in Portlyon. There she was, at age nine. Skinny legs in shorts and sandals. Age ten, on top of some rocks at the edge of Penlyon Cove. Eleven, running in a striped costume along the burning sands. Later, a teenager, looking wistful and quiet in a colour-block dress at sunset on the deck of the Loft. Her last summer in Portlyon for fifteen years.

The colour, the life, the brightness, and the love. This collection spoke of happiness, admiration, and inspiration. The notes in the sketchbooks bore this story out. 'Jessie at the harbour', 'Jessie at the

137

ice-cream parlour', 'Jessie – fishing', 'Jessica – asleep'. This last drawing, a delicate pen and ink rendering, clearly showed her likeness in quiet slumber. Her face was peppered with freckles from the summer sun.

Jess and Rob spent the rest of the day looking through the whole collection and making discoveries. Simon had been right. He had recalled the intense period of work before Kristof left Portlyon for France. This was when the paintings were completed, from his collection of sketches.

"He must have bricked them all up in this cavity," Rob examined the mortar and the space that Jess had opened up. "Then he asked me to repoint it here, and here."

"You remember doing it?"

"Yes," he put his hands on her shoulders, "but I had no clue that anything was *in* there."

She shook her head and smiled. "He was a cunning old devil, my father!"

27 BEGINNINGS

A wall of sound met the guests as they approached the Sailmaker's Loft. Motown hits and 1960s classics boomed out into the New Year's night.

Lyla and Fallon kissed passionately as they stabbed a knife into a lavish three-tier red velvet and passionfruit cake, carefully crafted by Gemma. The room full of friends and relatives erupted in loud cheering, camera phones blinked on and off to record it all. Lyla held her bouquet of pink and orange gerbera above her exquisitely coiffed bee-hive hairdo.
"Thank you all for coming! Now, let's party!!" She threw the bouquet into the crowd and the paper lanterns strung above their heads bobbed in response as the happy couple kissed once more.

The ceremony had been short and simple, touching and joyous. Everyone in the room knew they were meant for each other. Fallon stood with Rob at the front. Both looked fetching in matched waistcoats and cravats. Fallon had her usual smart quiff and bright brogues. Rob, more subdued, and handsome in his own quiet way. Lyla, escorted by her father, wore a specially made vintage-inspired couture dress. Lizbeth, seated with Alastair and Jess, nodded her approval.

Rob stood up as best man for his sister. He looked around at Jess and grinned. She smiled back at him. The look of love between them was as clear to everyone in the room as the love between the two brides. Alastair patted Jess's hand and gave it a gentle squeeze.

The couple spoke their self-penned vows. Rob had to hand Fallon a handkerchief as she tried to stammer out her words. The confident, blunt personality crumbled when confronted with the big day and her glowing, beautiful fiancée. Lyla was incandescent. Her jewellery had been her late mother's, her shoes were bespoke. Hollywood glamour come to Penlyon.

At the reception, Lyla called on Jess, Joanne, and Gemma to stand up and receive thanks for the delicious food and perfect cake. "My life changed in Portlyon," the beaming bride gushed her speech, "with my gorgeous wife, and the super-talented Jessica. I've gone from classroom to kitchen and I couldn't be happier."

In amongst the glinting red and white winter theme people ate and drank, talked, laughed, and danced. Glitter, confetti, and streamers festooned the room and fell gently over the guests. Lyla's white faux fur stole sparkled with a frosty coating. Warmth and celebration travelled throughout the room. After food and champagne came the fireworks. Up to the deck and into the courtyard went the guests to watch the display launched from the harbourside. Rob stood behind Jess, his arms around her, wrapping her in his muscular embrace. The coloured showers of light exploded above them in the dark, chilly sky, accompanied by 'Ooos' and 'Ahhhs' from the guests.

Only the day before, the first news of any comfort in a long time had reached Jess and Rob. Christy had finally been apprehended. She had hidden out with her sister who rapidly grew sick of her and called the police. The evidence against her was substantial. At first, she had tried to deny it all. But the police made it clear that it was a solid case. When they officially charged her, she decided to admit everything. There would be a harsh penalty to pay.

Jess and Rob had no time to think about this. The amazing find from behind the chimney at the Loft had changed all their plans and given Jess a whole new outlook and much to consider. A previously unknown cache of figurative, autobiographical works inspired by his daughter and Portlyon had brought about a craze for Kristof. The works were stored in the research and restoration rooms of the nearest large gallery in Cornwall that already owned a series of

Kristof's works. Carefully catalogued, they were destined to be examined by an eager tribe of experts.

There was no doubt about their authenticity and provenance. They were her father's work. She had invited Simon to see them, with Matty. The pictures of Jess included figures in the background. Simon was there, and Matty on her distinctive push-bike. Her vibrant hair was visible as she stood over a young Jess in her bright, striped swimsuit. As they scrutinised the pictorial history of Jess's summers, they could make out the name 'Carrie-Ann' on a vessel in the harbour. On board, Kristof had depicted two figures. Jess pointed them out to Rob. He held the canvas up carefully. They could clearly see a couple, the woman with dark hair, cropped close, a green blouse and shorts, beside her a bearded man in blue overalls.

"It's them," Rob's face had a nostalgic, happy expression, "Mum and Dad." He traced a finger over their outlines. Jess put her arm around him.
"It's yours," she kissed him.
He shook his head, "No, I can't accept this. It's a national treasure."
"It's yours. They are your family. These paintings are mine. I can do whatever I want with them and I give this one to you. Kristof left me The Loft and *all* its contents."
"It's ours," he came back, "our family."

With Simon and Matty, they worked through the beautiful, heartfelt drawings and paintings, and located themselves and other people they recognised. Simon, drawn in pen, on the old swivel chair in his shop surrounded by books. Matty, cycling down the lane, a spotted scarf flapping in the breeze from the harbour. Her tousled henna curls a shock of bright colour in the heart of the composition.

And Jess, different sizes, different ages. Beside the sea and on the deck. In the Sailmaker's Yard with an ice lolly and bucket and spade. In the background, the part-painted wooden steps and a skinny boy wearing dungarees up a ladder. Jess and Rob, in the same place, frozen in childhood together.

Up on the deck, after the guests had drifted and mingled their way back inside for dancing and the countdown to midnight, Rob and Jess stayed outside together. They kept each other warm in an embrace. Jess pulled up the collar of his jacket.
"It's cold, let's go inside."
"Wait, a couple of minutes. Can we?" He hugged her closer. "I want you to myself for the rest of the year, at least."
"Ok," and they kissed tenderly. She rested against his chest. "Who would have thought?" she smiled and breathed in his scent. "Who would have thought that those two kids would find each other after so many years and fall madly in love?"

Downstairs, voices chanted in unison, "Ten, nine, eight, seven, …".

Rob kissed her lips, passionately.
"Will you stay with me, always?" He looked intensely at her. Her pale blue eyes reflected in his dark, inky eyes.
"Of course," she returned his gaze, sincerely, seriously.
"Then, marry me?"

From downstairs, "Three, two, one, …", and then cheers to raise the roof.

Jess grinned from ear to ear. Before she could say anything, he presented her with a beautiful topaz and diamond ring. "My mother's. It wasn't lost in the fire because I had it with me that night. I was going to ask you then, as soon as you came back from London. But, we were – interrupted. What do you say?" He looked nervous, but he did not need to be.

As the townhall clock of Portlyon chimed in the New Year, Jess Trelawny, with tears of joy in her eyes, nodded, "Yes."

ABOUT THE AUTHOR

Amelia Blythe Robinson lives in the South West of England with her husband, two sons, and two cats. She began writing ten years ago, after years as an editor and researcher, and has produced non-fiction, reviews, and scripts for animation and children's theatre. *Return to Portlyon* is her first romance novel and is the first in a planned series dedicated to the fictional town on the Cornish coast.